# FLETCH

## THE CHAOS DEMONS MC

# NICOLA JANE

**FLETCH**
**The Chaos Demons MC**
**By**
**Nicola Jane**
Copyright © 2024 by Nicola Jane.

All rights are reserved.
No part of this
book may be used or reproduced in any manner without written permission from the author,
except in the case of brief quotations used in articles or reviews.
For information, contact Nicola Jane.

This book is a work of fiction. The names, characters, places, and incidents are all products of the author's imagination and are not to be construed as real. Any similarities are entirely coincidental.

Cover Designer: Wingfield Designs
Editor: Rebecca Vazquez, Dark Syde Books
Proofreader: Jackie Ziegler, Dark Syde Books
Formatting: Sienna Grant @V.R Formatting

# Spelling Note

Please note, this author resides in the United Kingdom and is using British English. Therefore, some words may be viewed as incorrect or spelled incorrectly, however, they are not.

# Trigger Warning

This book contains **triggers** for **violence, explicit scenes,** and some dirty-talking bikers. If any of this offends you, put your concerns in writing to Axel, he'll get back to you . . . maybe.

# Acknowledgments

**Thank you to all my wonderful readers—you rock!**

# Playlist

Torn - Natalie Imbruglia
Iris – Goo Goo Dolls
Lovefool – The Cardigans
Wonderwall – Oasis
What's Up? – 4 Non Blondes
Would I Lie To You? – Charles & Eddie
Lies – McFly
I Had Some Help – Post Malone ft. Morgan Wallen
Last Night – Morgan Wallen
Style – Taylor Swift
The Night We Met – Lord Huron
When We Were Young – Adele
Ghost Town – Benson Boone
Like I'm Gonna Lose You – Jasmine Thompson
Apologize – OneRepublic
Turn Me On – Norah Jones

# CHAPTER 1
### Fletch

"Last on the agenda is . . ." Axel, my President, looks down at his notes, "a police raid. Expected anytime this weekend." He shrugs, looking up and scanning the brothers sitting around his table. "Any personal use found is on you."

"Get rid of everything," Grizz, our Vice President, cuts in. "They're looking for any excuse at the minute, and I'm fucking sick of it. Clear your rooms of anything that could get you a fine or even a warning."

"Any other business?" asks Axel.

"Actually, I need someone to help me at The Bar tonight for a private function," says Grizz. We all look away, avoiding eye contact. "It's a hen do, fifteen women, drunk, excited and—" My hand is already up, along with most of the other brothers, and Grizz laughs. "Fletch, I'll take you."

"He always gets the good jobs," Atlas complains, and I smirk. But we all know Grizz isn't picking me 'cause we get on well—he doesn't wanna leave me here unattended around his old lady, Luna. Not that I'd ever go there again now he's claimed her, but she was once a club girl, which means she's fucked her way around the club, and lord knows she was memorable. We were building a connection, one that was severed when Grizz decided to claim her.

He throws me a set of keys, and I catch them. "You head over and stock up. I gotta bathe Ivy and then I'll be over." We all know he never misses bathtime with his baby girl, so I stuff the keys in my pocket.

Axel slams the gavel on the table, indicating the end of church, and we all head out.

Atlas falls in step beside me. "I'll come help," he tells me with a wink.

---

I RESTOCK the fridges behind the bar while Atlas sits staring at his mobile. "You gonna help or what?"

He looks up. "I'm here for the drunk pussy, brother."

I roll my eyes and check my watch. It's almost opening. "You may as well open the door," I tell him, and he grins, jumping up to do as I've asked.

Three women enter first. They're already singing and swaying, which tells me the hen do already started. The middle woman has a 'Bride' sash on, so I give good eye contact and smile wide. "Welcome, ladies," I greet. "What can I get you?"

The bride-to-be slams her hands on the bar and bites her lower lip before winking and slurring, "Whatever you're offering."

I laugh, grabbing the bottle of Prosecco that was already on ice. "Bubbles?"

## FLETCH

A few more women enter, but my attention is firmly on the blonde bride. Something about that last night of freedom turns me on. Atlas joins me behind the bar and begins serving the second group while I take care of the first. I offer to carry their tray of drinks to a nearby table, and as I set it down and they take a seat, I turn the charm up a dial. "Anna, right?" I ask, handing the bride-to-be her drink. Luckily, I'd already checked the bookings. Grizz likes things to be personal so the customer feels important.

She picks out the raspberry floating on top and pops it in her mouth. "And you are?"

"Fletch."

She grins. "Fletch," she repeats, letting my name roll off her tongue, "are you married?"

I shake my head, lowering into a spare seat. "Don't believe in that shit."

"Amen to that," her friend says, leaning closer to get my attention.

Anna pulls her back by the arm. "Hey, this is my night, remember," she snaps, and her friend rolls her eyes and snatches a drink from the tray.

I grin. "Don't fight, ladies, there's plenty of me to go around."

"I bet," comes a woman's voice from behind. I glance up, and she's staring at her friend with her hands on her hips. Her sash reads 'Bridesmaid'. "She's getting married next month, so move on, lover boy."

I stand, unable to stop the grin. "Don't I know you?"

"I hope not," she mutters, taking my seat and turning her back to me. I head back to the bar, racking my brain to try to remember where I recognise her from.

By the time Grizz arrives, the rest of the party is

filling the bar and the karaoke is in full swing. He winces as he shrugs from his kutte and hangs it behind the bar. "Jesus, who's idea was it to put the machine on?"

"Atlas," I say, rolling my eyes. "They've paid the extra."

I spot the bridesmaid stepping out the bar, and I remove the tea-towel from my shoulder and hand it to Grizz. "Taking my break," I throw over my shoulder as I head out.

She looks up from her phone when she senses me and rolls her eyes in irritation. "I swear I know you."

She narrows her eyes. "You're actually serious, aren't you?" When I don't reply, she smirks. "We fucked."

"Shit," I say, smiling. "Right, makes sense. I never forget a pretty face."

She arches a brow. "Oh god, what the fuck did I see in you?" I'm sensing bitterness. "I bet you don't even remember my name."

"I've never been great with names," I admit, wincing. "Look, sorry if I've pissed you off. I didn't mean to offend—"

"Gemma," she snaps. I pause, trying to recall her and then it hits me.

"Gemma," I repeat. "Gemma Stone?"

"Fuck me, Fletch, has it really been that many women you can't remember me?"

I'm almost lost for words as I give my head a shake. "No, it's just I didn't recognise you." I glance down her body, taking in her womanly curves that definitely didn't exist when we were together. "You're so much—"

"Thinner?" she spits. "Prettier?"

I swallow the lump that seems to be lodged in my throat. "Just different," I mutter feebly.

She rolls her eyes again and stomps back inside. I let out a long breath and lean against the wall. "Fuck," I say out loud.

"You asking for one from God?" comes Atlas's voice.

I smirk. "I *am* God."

He laughs. "The bar's busy, get back in here to help us mere mortals."

I head back inside, and Gemma turns her back as I approach. I stop behind her. "Sorry," I repeat. "You took me by surprise." Just being this close is a stark reminder of what I gave up. She smells different. Her perfume's changed along with her body and the colour of her hair. Back then, she was a redhead. Now, she's dark brown. She was curvier too, not that I minded it, but she hated her curves. I'm so lost in thought, I don't realise she's turned to face me.

"I'm just here for my friend's hen night. I think we can avoid one another, don't you?" She runs her tongue over her lower lip, and I watch the move, wondering if she still tastes the same.

"Sure thing, Snap."

She narrows her eyes at my nickname for her, and I smirk before moving on towards the bar.

---

It's almost midnight and the only women left are the bride-to-be Anna, Gemma, and another bridesmaid, Kelly, who are all crammed in the toilet while Anna brings up the contents of her stomach.

Grizz left half an hour ago, along with Atlas, because I drew the short straw to lock up. I'm stacking the clean glasses when Gemma appears. She leans on the bar and watches me for a minute. "Her fiancé is on his way to collect her." I give a nod. "You were a hit with the girls though," she adds. I turn to her, and she gives a small smile. "You always were."

"About all that—"

She shakes her head and holds her hand out to cut me off. I notice the sparkle of the diamond on her finger and grab it, holding it closer so I can inspect the engagement ring. She blushes, tugging it back to her and covering it under her other hand. It doesn't surprise me she's engaged. In fact, I'm more surprised she isn't married already.

## Gemma

THERE'S A LONG, drawn-out silence as he rounds the bar. "When's the big day?" he asks.

I keep the ring hidden, unsure why I'm embarrassed he's seen it. "What about you?" I ask. "Married, single?"

He shrugs. "Single."

I'm not surprised. He's a man whore. He always was. "We should probably stand outside," I mutter. He steps in front of me, and I halt, staring up at him. He's so much bigger than I remember. He always had a good body—it's one of the reasons I was so body conscious around him—but now, he's ripped and in the body of a man. My fingers itch to trace the tattoos that ride up his skin and over his face.

He steps closer, and my breath catches as he raises a

hand to my cheek. "The one that got away," he whispers. I blink, not daring to say a word, as he lowers his mouth until I feel his warm breath against my lips. If I was to pout, we'd touch.

"Gemma, help me get her outside," comes a voice from the bathroom.

I step back, breaking the spell and rush to the bathroom. *I cannot go around kissing bikers . . . not anymore.*

---

I GET two hours sleep before my alarm shrieks. I groan, checking the time to find it's three a.m.

I jump in the shower to wake myself up. I'm glad I didn't bother to drink during Anna's hen night because this will be worth the sacrifice.

I dress quickly and grab my car keys before heading out.

The station is a hive of activity. Whenever anything crops up involving The Chaos Demons, people volunteer, so everyone wanted to be in on this early morning raid.

I wait in the conference room for my team to gather, and once I'm satisfied everyone has arrived, I take my place at the front. "Thanks for turning in early today," I begin. "For those who don't know, I'm Detective Inspector Gemma Stone and I'm leading the investigation into gang-related violence and drugs surrounding The Chaos Demons motorcycle gang. Operation Sapphire is only a month into its investigations, so this raid will be the first of many."

I bring up the screen from my laptop onto the large whiteboard which shows the clubhouse floor plan. "We'll enter here," I explain. "There's a piece of fencing that's been damaged, which means we can gain access here rather than alert them at the gate." I point to a side door. "Access here will be gained with the magic key. Our intelligence suggests this is the only door not strengthened. Then, we'll spread out into our teams to search. Detain anyone you find, but keep them exactly where they are so we can search their rooms. Any questions?" It remains quiet, and I smile. "Great, let's go get these fuckers."

We assemble into riot vans and head out the station. The ten-minute drive is tense, not because of nerves but excited energy. We all want to be the team that puts an end to the biker club.

We park just out of view from the club. We file out and make our way through the broken fencing and to the side door leading into the club's kitchen.

One of my officers holds the battering ram that will have this door open in seconds. I give the nod, and he whacks it against the door, which springs open with little effort.

We head inside, shouting to make ourselves heard as we each go in the direction of our search areas. I take the stairs two at a time, followed closely by Kay and Phil. I take a breath before shoving a bedroom door open and turning on the light.

Fletch sits up in surprise, rubbing sleep from his eyes, as the naked woman beside him groans, rolling onto her back and taking the sheets with her. Fletch frowns when his eyes land on me, and I can't help the satisfaction I feel. "Morning, sunshine," I greet breezily. "Up you get." I head to his side of the bed with my handcuffs. He sits, not bothering to cover his nakedness, and holds his hands out in front. *Of course, he's done this before—his record is a mile long.* I cuff him and pull him to stand. "Someone grab him some clothes," I bark.

Kay grins, snatching up a pair of discarded boxer shorts and kneeling before him so he can step into them. She tugs them up, and he winks at her. "Thanks."

I shove him extra hard towards the wall. "We're detaining you while we search the premises under section one-hundred seventeen of the Police and Criminal Evidence Act."

He rolls his eyes. "You made it then," he remarks. I ignore him as three uniformed officers enter the room and begin to search it. Phil has the naked woman in cuffs, although she's now wrapped in a man's shirt. "Does your boss know you were out partying last night?" he asks. "I hope you didn't drive here."

"I don't break the law," I mutter just loud enough for him to hear.

He grins. "Not how I remember things."

I shove him face first against the wall. "Stay quiet."

It only amuses him more. "Usually, you like it rough, Snap. Have the tables turned?"

"Shut the fuck up," I hiss.

"Now, now, constable."

"Detective Inspector," I say with a hint of pride.

"Wow. You really climbed those ranks, Snap. You do that all by yourself or did daddy help?"

"Someone hold on to this fucker," I shout, shoving him towards another officer.

# CHAPTER 2
**Fletch**

I stare down at my feet, trying to rein in the anger I'm feeling. *Detective Inspector. Fuck.* I always knew she'd make it. It was the reason I knew we'd never work. But I'd secretly hoped she'd made her own way in the world and not decided to live in her dad's shadow.

Her feet appear in my eye line, and I raise my head until I meet her glare. "I hope your officers are gonna tidy that up," I say, nodding at my bedroom, which is a complete mess.

"It looks tidier now than when we came in," she retorts, arching a brow.

"I take it you didn't find what you were looking for?"

"We will," she says with confidence. "You wanna know why?"

"Enlighten me," I say, keeping my tone bored.

"Because I'm good at what I do, Fletch. I'm gonna tear your little club apart piece by piece until each and every one of you is locked away."

I grin. "Is that right?"

"Enjoy the rest of your night . . . morning."

"I intend to," I mutter as she stalks away.

Another officer pulls me up from the ground and walks me downstairs to where the other brothers are. Axel looks at me, and I shake my head to let him know they didn't find anything. Gemma stops by Lexi. "You're the bent cop," she remarks, looking amused.

Lexi smirks. "Not bent, just not a copper anymore."

"Don't fucking speak to her," Axel barks, and an officer pushes him to sit down.

"Touchy," sneers Gemma. "His office next," she orders, and a few officers head that way.

"You're wasting your time," snaps Grizz.

"If I'm pissing you off," she replies, "which I think I am, then it's a job well done."

"What exactly are you looking for?" I ask.

"Anything associated with crime," she replies, staring down at her phone.

"So, you have no idea," I mutter, shaking my head.

It's another hour before everywhere is searched and nothing is found. We're uncuffed while Gemma fills out some paperwork, handing it over to Axel with a grin. "We'll be seeing you again soon."

Axel waits until they've cleared out before ordering everyone into church.

"At least they didn't find anything," I say as we sit in our usual seats.

"Not the fucking point," he spits. "I'm sick of them on our backs. While she's sniffing around, everything else stops."

There are a few groans from the men who probably have arrangements in place they'll now have to cancel. Luckily for me, I run the garage and everything there is legit. "How did you know that bitch?" demands Grizz, eyeing me. "I saw the way she avoided you and how you looked at her."

I sigh heavily. "She's an ex."

"Are you shitting me?" snaps Axel.

"From way before I joined the MC," I rush to add. "We were practically kids. I didn't know she'd even moved this way."

"Coincidence?" he demands.

"Completely," I reply. "She was at the hen do last night in The Bar, though."

"Christ," mutters Grizz. "Does she have a vendetta or anything?"

I shrug. "That's not an answer," snaps Axel.

I groan. "We didn't end on good terms."

"In what way?" he asks.

"Well, she wasn't taking a hint, so I had to make things clear."

"How exactly did you do that?" demands Grizz.

I glance down at my hands, picturing the hurt on Gemma's face the last time she saw me. "I screwed her best friend."

A few of the men laugh, but Axel doesn't look impressed. "And how did that go down?" he grits out.

"As you'd expect. Like a fucking lead balloon."

"Is she the type to target us because of what you did?"

I shake my head. "Nah," I reply. "She's all good. Besides, wouldn't she have already come for me by now?"

"Not if she didn't know where you were," Smoke points out.

"It wouldn't be hard to track me, I've been arrested enough times."

"Either way, she's not going away," mutters Grizz. "Any chance you can sweet talk her?"

I laugh. "She's made it clear how she feels about me," I reply.

"Wouldn't hurt to grovel a bit though," he adds.

I narrow my eyes. "You trying to punish me?"

He grins. "You know I like to see you squirm."

"He's got a point," Axel cuts in. "It wouldn't hurt to sort it out with her."

"She won't give a shit, Pres. It was ages ago, and besides, she's engaged."

"Brother, if I know anything about women, it's that they never get over anything like that. Now, go fucking apologise," he snaps.

### Gemma

THERE WASN'T one fucking thing at the club, not even a tenner's worth of weed. My superior glares at me while my father paces the room. "It's like they knew we were coming," I mutter feebly.

"Impossible," snaps my father. Everyone assumes I got to where I am because he's Chief of Police, but it's crap. He wouldn't give me a helping hand in anything, let alone a career where he feels I don't belong. *Women don't belong in power.* That's what he told me when I decided to go for the position of Sergeant. I did it anyway, moving well away from him and settling in Leeds. I worked my way up, not bothering to speak to him about my success because he'd only have pissed on my parade. Now, there's no hiding it.

When I turned up to interview for this position, he about shit his pants. And I'm certain I wasn't his first choice, not because I wasn't perfect for the role, but because he'd hate that I'd be proving him wrong. Luckily for me, I had plenty of people backing me, as well as a panel of eight other superior officers who clearly went against him.

"We knew there'd be a possibility they'd see us coming. Since Lexi Cooper, they've been hiding things much better. They're less cocky. We just keep up the pressure, and they'll slip up eventually," says Karen, my Chief Superintendent, and I give a nod. "Good work today. The plan went without a hitch. It just wasn't our day."

I get in my car and bang the steering wheel several times. "Fuckkkkk," I scream. "Fuck, fuck, fuck!" I was certain there'd be something in that clubhouse. They knew we were coming, and I don't give a fuck what my father says. They *must* have spies on the inside.

I start the engine, and it rumbles before dying. I groan, turning the key a second time. It splutters before coming to life, reminding me it's due an MOT. I'm almost home when the traffic lights turn red and my car dies again. I growl, turning the key and listening as the engine ticks over. "You piece of crap," I hiss when it refuses to start.

Glancing in my mirror at the long line of traffic, I wince as I put on the hazard lights before climbing out and opening the bonnet. I have no idea how to fix a car, but at least I can hide behind the hood until the traffic has cleared. The light changes to green and some cars begin to beep while others take their time to manoeuvre around me and into the second lane.

The rumble of motorbikes slows as they near me, and I

close my eyes briefly when I see two Chaos Demons slow beside me. Fletch removes his helmet and gives me a big grin. "Car trouble?"

"Nope, I just love holding up traffic."

His friend removes his helmet and he also looks smug. "Pity you don't know a good mechanic." They share a laugh.

"Don't let me hold you up," I mutter, slamming the bonnet.

"You want a lift?" asks Fletch.

"No."

"You got recovery?" his friend asks, and I sigh, giving my head a small shake. I meant to sort it last month and kept putting it off. Fletch replaces his helmet, and I narrow my eyes. *He's seriously just gonna leave me?* He steers his bike in front of my car, up onto the pavement, and onto the forecourt of a garage. I glare at the big sign reading 'Chaos Cars'. This must be God's way of pissing me off. "Oh, would you look at that," his friend says with a wink, "a garage."

"Yeah, well, thanks, but I can sort my own car out."

The biker shrugs and follows Fletch onto the forecourt. I watch as they dismount, then I pull out my mobile and call Peter, my fiancé. He answers on the fourth ring, but he sounds busy by his tone. "Yep?"

"Hey, it's me," I say, glancing around at the garage as both bikers are now pushing up the shutters on the front.

"I'm in a meeting," he says firmly.

"Right, it's just I've broken down."

"Jesus, Gemma," he spits, and I hear him moving around until a door opens and closes. "What did I say to you about upgrading that damn car?"

"Yeah, I know, but I love this car."

"It's a bloody hazard, and now, you've broken down. I'm calling the scrap guys to come and take it, and this weekend, we're going car shopping."

"I'd rather you just come help me."

"Help you?" he spits. "You realise I'm not a fucking mechanic, right?"

"I think it's the battery, I just need a jump start."

"Can't you ask someone passing?"

"I'm asking you," I hiss, trying to keep calm.

"I am at work," he spits, like I'm stupid. "Yah know what, your life is fucking chaos," he snaps, and I roll my eyes at the lecture I'm about to get. "Unless it's to do with that fucking job, you don't show any interest. I reminded you about the breakdown coverage, I told you to sort the car, and now look, you're calling me to come rescue you. Where are you?"

"I'll send you my location," I mutter, relieved to pull the phone away from my ear for a second's peace while I ping him.

"Are you kidding me?" he roars, and I wince at his tone. "You're right next to a fucking garage."

"I can't use them," I mumble, making sure to turn away in case Fletch is watching me. "We raided their place this morning."

"You better swallow that massive ego and ask them to look at your heap of shit car. I have an important job too." He disconnects, and I sigh heavily, turning back to face the garage.

I take a deep breath and shake out my shoulders before heading towards the small office connected to one side of the building. The rest is the workshop, and there are already two cars on the ramps.

I push open the door and step inside. Fletch looks up from the computer, and when he sees it's me, he looks back down and continues what he was doing.

"Erm," I sigh, "could you take a look at my car . . . please?"

He looks back to me, a smirk pulling at his lips. "We're busy."

"Right. When can you fit it in?"

He picks up a thick book and slams it on the counter. He opens it and stares at the bookings. "Maybe next week."

"Next week?" I almost screech.

He shrugs, slamming it closed again. "Sorry we couldn't help."

I growl. "Wait. Okay, fine. Next week is fine."

"It'll cost . . ." he adds, reopening the book and flicking through the pages.

"You don't even know what's wrong with it."

"I mean for the recovery."

I scoff. "It's right outside."

"Still . . . if it don't start, I gotta pay to have it moved onto the forecourt."

"You're taking the piss," I hiss.

"Like you were last night when you looked at me, begging me to kiss you."

I frown. "I was not."

He grins. "You forget, Snap, I know every inch of you, and I know what you wanted last night."

My eyebrows shoot up. "Are you kidding me?" I snap,

stepping closer to the counter and slamming my hands on top to fix him with a glare. "You didn't even recognise me last night, so you don't know every inch of me, not anymore."

"You're right," he admits, "we should fix that."

I pinch the bridge of my nose and shake my shoulders out again to try and get rid of the tension building there. "Look, Fletch, can you fix my car or not? If you're going to be a dick about it, I'll find someone else."

He shrugs. "Fine, take care."

I clench my jaw tightly. "But it would be easier if you could help me out."

"Tell you what, Snap . . ." I watch as he lifts the partition in the counter and steps through. "I'll make you a deal." I swallow hard as he fills my space, and I instinctively lower my eyes to the floor. I don't know why he makes me feel so nervous. I haven't felt butterflies in my stomach since . . . *him*. I sigh out loud. Fletch places his finger under my chin, and I inhale sharply at the contact. He lifts my head so I have no choice but to look him in the eye.

"I'll look at your car today and drop the recovery charge if you meet me later." I'm already shaking my head and thinking up a hundred reasons why I should refuse. "No one needs to know," he adds. "I just wanna catch up with you. Hell, bring the fiancé if it makes you feel better." I almost laugh at the thought of Peter meeting Fletch. He'd think I was having a mental breakdown.

"Fine. Where?" He grins, pulling out his mobile and looking at me expectantly. "I'm not giving you my number," I say, this time unable to stop the small laugh that escapes me. "Do you know how bad that will look, how any of this will look?" I take a step back, allowing my brain to kick in and rescue me. "Eight o' clock at Miller's Barn Bar. A minute late and I'm gone," I say firmly.

He smirks again, and this time, it irritates me. "I only needed your number for the records," he says, nodding towards the book on the desk. "So we can call you when the car is ready."

Embarrassment creeps up over my cheeks, but I give a slight nod, snatching his mobile and quickly inputting my number. "Fine. There." I hand it back. "For car discussions only."

He bites his lower lip, that smile still in place. "Of course. Tonight, eight."

# CHAPTER 3

**Fletch**

Luna gently rocks Ivy in her arms, and I allow my eyes to run down her body, remembering how those tanned legs looked wrapped around me. I give my head a shake, and she glances up. "So, is it a real date or just fake?"

I take a sip of my whiskey. "Fake. Why the fuck would I want to date a copper?"

"You're dressed smart," she remarks, smirking.

I glance down at the plain black T-shirt that clings to my toned chest. It's one of many I own, but they're always hidden under my kutte, which for one night only, I've hung up at Grizz's command. I don't want to draw extra attention to Gemma and spook her before I've had a chance to work my magic. "I need her to take me seriously."

"Sure," she says, winking. "And there's not a small part of you hoping to get laid."

I laugh. "Been there, done that, and if I remember right, she wasn't that great." It's a lie I've told myself to stop me wanting her. Cos since she strolled into The Bar last night, she's all I've thought about.

"Shouldn't you be dating a pig right about now?" snaps Grizz as he crosses the room towards us, wrapping his arm protectively around Luna. She smiles up at him with complete love, and I want to smack him upside the head for thinking she'd ever look in my direction when she's completely smitten with him.

I push to stand. "Just on my way, VP."

---

MILLER'S BARN is in a quieter part of town, and when I step inside, I spot Gemma seated towards the back nursing a glass of lemonade. I roll my eyes and head for the bar to order two whiskeys.

When I sit down and place one of them in front of her, she startles. "Hey," I say, smiling and nodding at the drink. "Peace offering?"

"I don't . . . I'm not drinking."

"You used to love a whiskey," I point out, sipping my own.

"Used to," she mutters, staring into her lemonade.

"It's been a while, Snap."

She sighs, tipping her head to one side and bringing her eyes to meet my own. "Stop calling me that. And it's been fourteen years."

"Jesus," I say, releasing a long breath, "no wonder I didn't recognise you."

"I haven't changed that much," she mumbles, swirling her drink in the tumbler.

"Oh, you have, Snap, so much."

"You're right," she agrees. "I'm an adult now, and I don't take crap or fall for bullshit lines. Now, get to the point. Why did you want to meet?"

I lean back and frown. "Still so feisty."

"Because if you thought you could sweet talk me into laying off your club, you're wrong."

I hold my hands up in surrender. "There's no ulterior motive here, Gem. Just an old friend wanting to catch up."

"There's always an ulterior motive with you, Fletch." She snatches up the whiskey and takes a drink, wincing before placing it back on the table.

"So, you're getting married? When, and who's the lucky fella?"

"I'm not feeding you information on me," she snaps.

I roll my eyes. "Jesus, you're still paranoid, aren't yah?"

She scowls. "I was right to be paranoid all those years ago, wasn't I?"

"You accused me so much that in the end I thought I may as well do it if I was gonna get blamed anyway."

She shakes her head in disappointment and pushes to stand. "This was a bad idea."

I groan, grabbing her wrist. "Wait. Sorry. Please don't go." She hesitates but slowly lowers to sit again. "I was a prick back then. I treated you like shit and . . . well, I don't have an excuse, just that I was young and stupid. I'm sorry I treated you like that, Gemma. I truly am."

She visibly swallows and gives a slight nod to acknowledge my apology. "Never thought I'd hear an apology slip from the lips of the great Cam Fletcher," she mutters, taking another sip of the whiskey.

"Thought you weren't drinking," I say, tipping my glass to hers and lightly tapping it. "Here's to forgiveness?"

She scoffs. "Here's to a long overdue apology. Forgiveness has to be earned."

"Is that an offer for me to try?"

"So, you're not married. How come?" she asks, changing the subject.

"Guess I never found the right one," I tell her, shrugging. "Besides, who wants to get involved with guys like me?"

"Are you referring to the biker part or criminal?"

"Are they separate?" I ask, and she presses her lips into a fine line in that way cops do when they're avoiding talking so you'll feel uncomfortable enough to keep talking and maybe slip up. "I did my time, Gemma. These days, I'm running in cleaner circles."

"With The Chaos Demons?" she asks, her tone mocking. "Please, don't feed me your bullshit, Cam. We're not on a first date, and you can't blind me with lies."

"It's Fletch," I tell her, "and if you're so sure about us, how come I'm not in the cells right now?"

"You knew we were coming," she replies cooly. "That's why there was a gap in the fence, and why we got in on the first hit on what was supposed to be an enforced door. We were guided to that entrance, and it's why the club was clear of anything."

I rest my elbows on the table and fix her with a confident stare. "I don't know what you expected to find, officer, but as I've already said, I run in clean circles these days."

"I'm getting married in a few months," she admits, leaning back and breaking the tension that was beginning to build. "We opted for a winter wedding at the castle."

"Cliché," I reply, draining my drink.

"He's amazing," she coos. "Good job, stable, the perfect man."

I grin. "Sounds it."

"He's a surgeon, in case you were wondering."

"I wasn't."

"And he doesn't give my friends a second look. I can trust him around them."

"Good for you."

"Do you have contact with her?" she asks, suddenly looking less confident.

I shake my head, knowing instantly she's referring to Kate, the woman I fucked behind her back. "We weren't a thing." She rolls her eyes. "Seriously," I reassure her, "we weren't a thing. It was a one-off, which I came to regret."

"Sure."

"Do you still see her?"

"Sometimes," she admits. "She's related to my fiancé."

"Oh," I say, surprised. "Weird."

"Not really. I was friends with Kate for a long time, and when everything happened with you and her, Pete was there for me."

"Pete?" I repeat, racking my brain to fit a face to that name. My eyes widen. "Her brother?"

"Half-brother," she corrects.

"He was a wanker," I point out.

"He just never liked you. Can't say I blame him."

I grin. "Pete's a surgeon? Wow. Who did he screw to get there?"

She narrows her eyes. "Actually, he's a damn good one and he worked his backside off to get there."

I'm amused and I can't hide it. Back then, she couldn't stand Pete. He was arrogant and self-assured. He'd always put both girls down, especially Gemma. "Did you tell him about me and Kate?"

"Of course. He didn't speak to her for years."

"What a hero."

"Because he respected me," she hisses, "and was disgusted she'd do that to her best friend."

"So, you and he got together after that?" She begins picking at a paper napkin and it's my turn to narrow my eyes. "What are you hiding?"

"We were flirting way before then," she admits, and my mouth falls open. "You were being a dick, and he was there." She shrugs. "He was nice to me."

"So, you've been together for, what, over fourteen years?"

She shakes her head. "No. We were getting close and . . . well, I had to go away for a while. We stayed in touch, and when I returned briefly, we had a thing, but with him at university and me in the police cadets, it took us a while to get together."

"Why did you go away?"

"My father," she mutters. "He thought it would be best." She takes a breath and releases it slowly. "Anyway, I've been with Pete for three years."

"And now, you're at the top?" I add.

"Not the top, that would be taking my father's job," she adds a laugh, "but I'm where I want to be for now."

"What happened to the dream of opening your own shop and selling flowers?"

She smiles, and for the first time, it lights her blue eyes. "You remember that, huh?"

"Of course. You loved flowers and opening a shop was

your dream. You were gonna tell your dad, if I remember right?"

Her smile fades. "Well, reality set in and I realised flowers wouldn't pay the bills."

I frown. "So, what happened to that huge plot you rented and filled with bright flowers?" She'd saved money from her part-time job at sixteen to rent an allotment space so she could grow her plants. Her father didn't know about it, and it was the one place she loved to be, spending all her free time there. It's how we hid our two-year relationship from him, often meeting up there.

"I grew up," she says.

I frown. "Bullshit. You don't stop enjoying stuff like that. You loved that place."

Sadness passes over her. "He found out," she admits. "He made me pull them up."

"What?"

"My father."

"Gemma, I'm—" She cuts me off before I can say how sorry I am. He was always a prick, from what she'd told me.

"It's fine. It was for the best. Besides, I went away for a year, so my plants would've died anyway."

"I bet you have a garden full of colour now to make up for it?"

She gives a slight shake of her head. "Pete hates flowers. He gets terrible hay fever, and we chose a place with a tiny garden. Low maintenance."

"You don't have a garden?"

"Does it matter?" she suddenly snaps. "My father only found out about the bloody garden because of you."

"Me?"

"He read my text messages. You talked about meeting there."

"He must be pleased you're a cop," I say, changing the heavy subject.

She gives an empty laugh. "He's not pleased no matter what I do. Anyway, what about you? Tell me about your life now."

I scrub a hand over my nine o'clock shadow. "I work the garage and sometimes help the brothers in their businesses."

"Yeah, I saw the Demons own a few."

"All legit," I tell her. "Where is lover boy tonight, anyway?" I ask. "Doesn't he mind you meeting a biker for a drink?"

"He's working late," she says, and there's something in her eyes that tells me she's not happy about it.

"You didn't tell him you bumped into me?"

"Why would I? It's not important."

I grin. "I was your first love. In fact, I was your first for other things too. I'd want to know if it were me."

Her phone rings out before she can reply and she startles, grabbing it from her bag. She fiddles for a second, and I realise she was recording. I smirk, pushing to stand. "You take care, Snap. It was good to see you."

She glances from her phone to me. "Wait," she says, cancelling the call. I head for the exit, and she rushes behind. "Fletch," she calls as I step out of the bar, "wait."

I turn quickly, and she comes to an abrupt stop, almost crashing into my chest. She visibly swallows, but I know she's not scared of me. It's something else behind those baby blues, lust maybe. I crowd her as she backs up until she hits the wall, then I place a hand above her head and lean in close.

"What do you want, Snap?" I whisper, and her eyes are fixed to my mouth again. "You think I'm gonna sit there and confess all? You might be the first virgin I ever fucked, but you're still a pig."

My words break the spell, and she gives her head a slight shake. "Step away from me, Cameron," she says firmly.

I ignore her, moving closer still until my cheek brushes hers, and she inhales sharply. "I'll call you about the car," I murmur close to her ear, using my free hand to wrap a lock of her brown hair around my finger. "It was good to catch up." I push off the wall and walk away, refusing to look back, because as much as I want to, I cannot get involved with Gemma Stone.

**Gemma**

I WATCH HIM LEAVE, shuddering as the warmth goes from my body. *Fuck.* He's still a smooth bastard. My phone rings out again, and I jump with fright, accepting the call and walking in the opposite direction. "Yep?"

"How did it go?" asks Phil.

"He's too guarded. We covered old ground, but he gave me nothing."

"Did we expect him to?" he asks. "You coming in?"

"On my way," I mutter, disconnecting and flagging down a passing taxi.

I get to the station five minutes later, and Phil is

already updating Karen as I join them in her office. It feels lighter now my father isn't pacing the floor. "Tell me from the beginning," she says firmly, her brows pinched together in that worried way I often see when I stumble across an 'opportunity' without running it by her. I can't blame her. She was the superintendent when Lexi Cooper fucked up and ran off with the club's president, so she gets nervous when operations have anything to do with the club.

"It was an accident," I tell her, and she rolls her eyes. "I swear," I add. "My car broke down outside his garage."

"You didn't even tell me there was a history there," she snaps.

"I didn't know it was him," I argue. "Not until I saw him in The Bar." She glares, and I sigh. "I was out on my friend's hen night, and he was working in there, wearing one of their kuttes. I haven't seen him for years and I didn't know his circle was gonna be the club we were watching."

"What's his history?" she asks, standing and passing us to go into the boardroom next to hers. We follow, and she slides a pen and a bunch of Post-it notes towards me. I take them and sit at the large table.

"His name is Cameron Fletcher," I say as I write it down. "The badge on his kutte said 'Enforcer'." I write that underneath and take it from the pad to pass to Phil, who sticks it on the board along with the names of all the other Chaos Demons members. "He's originally from Nottingham. That's where I met him when I was sixteen," I continue, feeling uneasy as I relay some of my personal life. "We were just kids, but even then, he was trouble. He was in with a bad crowd, selling drugs, drinking. No parents that I know of and there are no siblings. He's not married and no kids." I scribble the garage name on the second Post-it. "He runs Chaos Cars."

"Which is where your car is?" she asks, and I nod. "And what was tonight?"

I shrug. "A catch-up."

"With a criminal you're actively investigating?"

"I saw it as an opportunity."

"You didn't run it by me," she yells, slamming her hand on the table. "Which means even if he confessed his deepest, darkest sins, we wouldn't have been able to use them in court because a decent judge would've thrown it out and accused us of entrapment."

"I'm sorry," I mutter. "There wasn't time."

"Bullshit, Gemma. Don't pull a stunt like that again or I will take you off the case." She turns away to look out the window. "In fact, I might take you off it anyway."

"No," I say a little too loudly. She turns to face me, and I swallow the panic. "I've worked hard on this," I tell her. "Please don't pull me."

"What was your relationship with him?"

"I was a kid," I repeat. "It was a stupid crush, nothing important. He didn't even recognise me right away. Please . . . we can use this to our advantage."

"Not a chance," she snaps. "I'm not losing another good officer to that club. From now on, you run everything by me."

I nod, and as she heads for the door, I exchange a look with Phil that tells him I'm going to push my luck. He knows me well enough now and lets out a groan. "Actually," I add, and she slows, "I really believe he'll be my way in."

"How?"

"He was flirting."

She groans too as I stand. "Just hear me out. What if we can get it approved for me to pursue this?"

"I just told you no."

"I won't get into a relationship with him," I reassure her. "I'll do it right."

"Like Lexi Cooper?" she throws at me.

"I'm not like her. She was a rookie. I can do this. Let me get friendly and see what I can find out."

She scrubs her hands over her tired face. "It won't work. He'll never let his guard down with you because he knows who you are."

"I can spin it to make him think I'm like the old me."

"And who exactly was that?" she demands.

"A carefree, flower-loving kid who didn't want to follow in her father's footsteps."

"You know I have to run this by him."

"Fine," I mutter, shrugging and praying he doesn't recognise the name. "Without all the detail?" I ask hopefully. "I don't think my father needs to know about sixteen-year-old me falling for a biker." Even though he already knows in way more depth than that.

Karen pulls open the door and leaves. I flop down into a chair as Phil sits opposite me. "He'll never agree."

"Of course, he won't. Anything to stop me looking good."

I WAKE WITH A START. I left the station at midnight and Peter still wasn't home, so I'd fallen to sleep on the couch. Groaning, I push to sit as my muscles ache in protest. I grab my phone to check the time and see three missed calls from my father.

If I'm going to hear a lecture, I at least need caffeine, so I head for the kitchen and turn on the kettle. But before I've even grabbed a cup, it rings again, and I growl in frustration before answering. "Good morning," I say brightly. "I was just about to return your calls."

"It's almost ten in the morning and you've only just woken up," he barks.

"I pulled an eighteen-hour shift yesterday and still went back last night to speak to my super."

"Cameron Fletcher," he barks, and I wince. It was too much to hope he'd forgotten that name after everything.

"It's a good opportunity," I say.

"For you to go crawling back?"

"Don't be ridiculous, I'm practically married. I was a child when I last knew him."

"I want you off the case," he says firmly.

"No," I snap. "Don't you dare."

"It's my decision."

"A bad one," I yell angrily. "You hate that I might actually succeed."

"Don't be ridiculous."

"I can take down this club, and you know I can. Let me do this and it'll make you front page."

"Are you forgetting what he did?" he hisses.

"How can I when you refuse to let me forget?" I spit. "I hate him, and that makes me the perfect candidate for this. I *will* take down The Chaos Demons. Please don't stand in my way."

There's silence on his end, and I hold my breath. "Fine, but you will come and see me regularly with updates." It's a way for him to feel in control, so I reluctantly agree.

# CHAPTER 4

### Fletch

I zone out while Axel fumes about the raid the other night. "Fletch," snaps Grizz, nudging me.

"Huh?" I ask, breaking from my thoughts of Gemma.

Axel is glaring at me. "Nyx mentioned you took the copper's car in at the garage."

I nod. "Yep. She broke down right outside. How's that for sod's law?"

"You think she did it on purpose, or it was for real?" asks Smoke.

"Nah, it's fucked, not even roadworthy. I met her for a drink too." I feel Axel's eyes burning into me. "What?" I ask innocently. "You told me to apologise to her, soften her up."

"Did she give anything up?" asks Grizz.

I shake my head. "Of course not. Although I did find out her father is Chief of Police."

"Mark Stone?" Grizz questions.

"Isn't he the new one?" asks Smoke, and Axel nods.

"A right miserable fucker, apparently," says Grizz

"Not interested in meeting us to discuss anything. He's nothing like the last guy."

"I never met the man, but she was terrified of him back then," I tell them. "We'd meet in secret."

"Man, if I was dating someone as ugly as you, I'd keep it secret too," jokes Ink.

"What's the plan here?" asks Axel.

"You tell me," I say. "You and the VP told me to make things right. I did."

"You think she'd spill secrets?" asks Grizz.

"I doubt it, brother. She doesn't seem the type to break rules these days."

"These days?" repeats Axel. "Which means she used to?"

I grin. "She was a rebellious teen, what do you think?"

"Find that inner rebellious streak and break it. We need her off our backs."

I salute him as he bangs the gavel on the table and then I head out.

Grabbing my phone from my pocket, I dial Gemma and she answers on the second ring. "It's Fletch," I tell her. "It's about the car."

"Right," she whispers, "hold on." I hear her moving and then a door open and close. "Okay, hit me with it."

"I don't think you'll be surprised to know it's not good news."

"You can't fix it?" She sounds disappointed.

"I didn't say that. I'm a good mechanic, I can fix anything, but it's an old car and probably not worth putting the new parts in. For what you'll spend, you could get a new car."

"Really?"

"Gem, it ain't worth shit. Scrap it, you'll make more."

She sighs heavily. "I can't do that. It's sentimental."

"A car?" I ask, laughing. "Take a picture, it'll last longer and cost nothing."

"Is that about the car?" barks a man's voice. It's harsh, and she doesn't even answer before he's clearly taken the phone from her. "Hi, I'm Gemma's husband. If you're feeding her some crap about fixing that heap of junk, save it."

"Actually," I say, frowning, "I was just telling her it's not worth spending the money on it."

"Right," he mutters. "Well, good. We've had enough mechanics rip her off. She's holding on to it for dear life, and it's time she let it go."

"I'm right here," I hear her mutter.

"So, scrap it," he continues.

"Pete," she screeches, "give me the phone."

"I'll handle it, Gem."

"Actually, sir," I say clearly, "your wife is the customer, so I'll need to speak to her about it. And I'm not a scrap man. You'll need to arrange that yourself."

Gemma comes back onto the line. "Sorry about that. Are you in the garage now?"

"Just about to head that way," I tell her. "You want me to pick you up?"

"Erm . . ." She's hesitant, and I imagine it's because her fiancé is nearby. "Same place as before?"

"Miller's Barn?"

"Yep, great. Thank you." It reminds me of our secret conversations when she was younger and didn't want her father to overhear. I disconnect and head out to my bike.

# FLETCH

I SLOW OUTSIDE THE BAR, where she's standing waiting. She eyes the bike as I hand her the spare helmet. "I've never . . ." I take the helmet from her and push it on her head, pulling her closer so I can fasten the chin strap.

"Climb on," I order, and she slides on behind me. "Feet there," I say, tapping her ankles and guiding them to the footrests. "Hold on and move with me." Her hands grab my kutte, and I smirk, taking them and tugging them until she's so close, I can feel her heat at my back. "Hold on," I repeat, revving the engine and turning back out into traffic.

It's a short ride to the garage but one of my best so far. Having Gemma this close, clinging to me, makes me hotter for her. The fact she's engaged to that cock makes things worse. My want is becoming a need.

We climb off, and she follows me to the office. I unlock it, and we go inside. "Nice to hear he's changed."

"Huh?"

"Your fiancé," I say, lifting the partition and stepping behind the counter.

"Oh," she gives a small laugh, "he just hates that car."

"It's a death trap, and I agree it needs scrapping."

She folds her arms over her chest. "It was my first car," she admits. "I know it's stupid to get attached, but I got it with my first wage from the force."

"Snap, I know your father is loaded, so why did you buy that heap?"

"I'd never ask him for anything," she mutters. "But you're right, I know you are, so I'll get a scrap man to collect it."

"I'll deal with it," I say.

"You sure?"

I give a nod. It's the least I can do, and she's clearly struggling to let it go. "You want to empty it?" I ask, and she nods. "Come," I say, unlocking the side door that leads into the workshop. "I've got some boxes too," I tell her, grabbing a couple from a shelf.

She unlocks the car and slides into the driver's seat. I open the passenger side and get in. "It's a cute little car," I say. "I took you for more of an Audi kind of girl."

"Really?" she asks, arching a brow. "I got the Mini Cooper because my father hated them," she admits, and I laugh.

"You were always trying to rebel. What's he think of the surgeon?"

"Loves him," she almost whispers. "They get on really well."

I frown. "Strange."

"Is it?"

"That you'd meet a man who gets along with your father, yeah. What do you think he'd make of me?"

She grins, resting her head back but keeping her eyes trained on me. "He hates tattoos."

I smirk. "I bet he does."

"The fact they're on your face would send him over the edge."

"Yeah, a nice addition, don't you think?"

Her hand reaches out, brushing over my cheek. "Is it true what they say?" I wait for her to continue, enjoying the soft touch of her fingers as they trace my tatts. "Do these represent the people you've killed?"

I twist my head from her touch, and her hand drops to her lap. "I'll let you pack your shit up." It's easy to forget the real reason she's acting all nice, but she never fails to remind me.

I climb from the car, slamming the door and heading back to the office.

Half an hour passes before she reappears. I'm already with a customer, so she takes a seat as I rip off the receipt and hand it to the blonde who's spent the last ten minutes flirting. Any other day, I'd probably have her out back sucking my cock, but something about having Gemma here puts me off.

"So, that number?" she repeats, taking the receipt.

I glance at Gemma, who quickly looks away. "Sure," I mutter, grabbing a business card and scribbling my number on the back before handing it to her.

I wait for her to leave before lifting the partition and stepping through to where Gemma sits. "I called the scrap man. He's gonna give you two hundred."

"Wow, is that it?"

"Take it or leave it."

"I'll take it. I'm just waiting for a ride home," she says. "I left the boxes in the garage," she adds. "I didn't realise how much crap I kept in the car." She stands. "It's the perfect business . . . for meeting women."

I stare out the window, watching the blonde who is now chatting to Nyx, and I smirk. "Free and single these days, remember."

"I wasn't . . . judging. I'm just saying it's surprising you're still single when there are women throwing themselves at you like that."

"There was a time when I'd have taken her out back," I mutter. "Probably with Nyx," I admit. "But . . ." I shake my head. "Never mind."

Gemma steps closer. "Thanks for all your help with the car."

"Am I likely to see you again?" I ask.

She smirks. "Depends."

"On?"

"If your club is as clean as you say it is."

"You're wasting your time," I tell her. "The last copper who thought she could take us down ended up becoming part of the club." I close the gap between us, and she tips her head back to look up at me.

"I'm not her," she whispers, her eyes burning with need.

I run my lower lip through my teeth, and before I can change my mind, I kiss her. It's soft, and although she hesitates, the second I wrap my hand around her throat, she relaxes and allows my tongue to explore her mouth. It's a few seconds before she comes to her senses and pushes me back. "What the fuck are you doing?" she snaps.

"What you wanted," I tell her, smirking.

"I didn't want that," she spits. "I'm getting married."

A car horn beeps, and she spins to look outside at a sleek, shiny BMW. I grin. Of course, he drives a dick's car. "Your chariot awaits."

"Don't fucking come near me again," she warns, stomping off out the exit. I open the side door and lean against the frame, watching as she scoops one of the boxes into her arms. "You want me to help? Cos it doesn't look like lover boy is gonna."

"I can manage," she hisses, carrying it out towards the car. The boot opens automatically, and she dumps it in before heading back towards me.

"What a catch. Does he slam doors in your face too?"

"Don't be a prick."

"I'm not the one watching my fiancée haul boxes around. Is it his hands he's protecting?"

She pauses in front of me. "He's worth ten of you."

I smile. "Ten? Wow."

"What do I owe you for looking at the car?"

"Nothing, sweetheart. That kiss was more than enough."

She scoffs. "You're a prick." And she stomps back towards the car.

"Never claimed to have changed," I call after her before storming into the office and slamming the door closed.

Seconds later, Nyx follows me in. "What the hell's wrong with you?"

"I kissed her," I blurt, and he arches a brow.

"Was that the plan?"

I run my hands through my hair in agitation. "What fucking plan? There is no plan, but I just kissed her and, fuck, I . . . I enjoyed it way more than I should have."

"You're overthinking. What's this chick got that all the club whores don't have? Nothing," he says firmly. "Go fuck someone else and forget about her. She's a copper, and we don't mix with that sort."

I give a stiff nod and crack my neck from side to side. He's right—Gemma is old news, and before this week, I hadn't thought of her in years.

**Gemma**

"How much did they rob you?" asks Peter as he pulls out into traffic.

I stare straight ahead, my mind racing from what just happened. The kiss felt . . . nice. I scrub my hands over my face. *Who the fuck am I kidding?* The kiss was hot and made me feel like a goddamn teenager again. I growl, and Peter laughs, glancing over at me. "That much, huh? Told you they'd rip you off."

"Where were you all night?" I ask, sounding harsher than I mean too.

"Working, like always. Why?"

I sigh heavily. "Nothing. It's just, well, you're working a lot lately."

I feel his eyes on me briefly. "I'm a fucking surgeon, Gem. I work when I'm needed, and last night, I was needed."

"And was she on shift?" I brace myself for the temper tantrum I know will follow. It always does when I mention his past affairs.

He doesn't disappoint me, slamming his hands on the steering wheel. "Why does it always come back to her?" he yells angrily.

"Well, because I can't help but be curious when you're gone all night. It brings back memories," I snap. He slams his foot down, swerving in and out of traffic and causing other vehicles to beep at us. "Slow down," I hiss.

"I'm so fucking tired of hearing it, Gemma. You said you'd forgiven me. I thought we'd moved on."

"We have," I mutter, gripping the door handle of the car as he swerves to avoid a vehicle slowing in front. "Please, Pete, slow down."

"Scared one of your colleagues will pull us over?" he sneers.

"Well, you'll get the ticket," I retort.

"All you care about is that job and your image."

I narrow my eyes. "You're one to talk." He turns onto our road, and I let out a sigh of relief. "And don't think I didn't realise you never answered me."

He pulls onto the drive, pressing for the garage door to open. I frown when he turns off the car engine and climbs out. I follow his lead, wondering why he doesn't put the car away, and pause when I see a new car already in its spot with a huge ribbon on the bonnet.

"Yes, Gemma," he hisses, "Carla was on shift. Did we fuck? No. Did we even speak? No. Because you made it quite clear what would happen if I did." I keep my eyes on the white BMW, its red ribbon blowing gently in the breeze. "I'm tired of going over the same shit, Gem." I notice just how exhausted he sounds. "And by the way, I got you a car." Then, he stomps up the steps and into the house, slamming the door behind him.

I go into the garage and run my hand over the shiny paintwork. *I hate white cars.* I laugh to myself, allowing a tear to roll down my cheek. *And I fucking hate BMWs.*

When I go inside, I hear Peter upstairs. "I love the car," I call out, slipping off my shoes and dumping my bag. I head upstairs to find him in the shower. "I said, I love the car."

"Liar, you hate BMWs." It begs the question why he'd buy me one if he already knew that.

I lean in the doorway and smile. "I like that one because you got it for me."

"We have dinner with your father in an hour," he

informs me, and I groan. "He called last minute, so I couldn't say no."

I go into the bedroom. "You could. It's an easy word."

I pull my shirt over my head and drop it on the bed just as Pete's phone flashes with a text message. I bite my lower lip and glance back towards the bathroom. The shower is still running, so I quickly go over to his bedside table and stare at the screen. I shouldn't check it. I haven't done it for so long, not since I first found out about his affair with a nurse at work. It lights up again, and the fact he has it on silent makes me more suspicious. My hand hovers over it, and I groan, snatching it up and opening it. There are two text messages, and as I scan them, my heart breaks all over again.

> C: I can get out at ten tonight.

> C: Maybe we can get some food and then I can treat you ;)

Tears fill my eyes as a third message comes through. The picture of silk underwear laying on a bed mocks me, and I don't even realise the shower has turned off until Pete's voice fills the room. "What are you doing?" he asks.

I turn to him with silent tears rolling down my cheeks. "You didn't even have the decency to come up with a better name," I whisper, and his expression changes from confused to guilty. "What was the plan? You'd get called away from dinner, leaving me to face that bastard alone?"

"Gem," he mutters, his tone pleading.

"Why couldn't you just be honest?" I ask, dropping his phone onto the bed. "You could've just left the first time, but you asked . . . no, you begged for me to give you another chance, and again, I did."

"I tried to stop," he explains.

"But she was just too tempting."

"I'm sorry."

"Oh god, you're so fucking pathetic when you're ridden with guilt. Get the fuck out."

"What?"

"You heard me, get the fuck out of my house."

"We're getting married. Come on, don't act crazy."

My eyes widen. "Are you serious? Get the hell out!" I march over to his wardrobe and pull it open. His clothes are hanging neatly and it pisses me off. He's always so fucking tidy. I begin to rip them from the hangers and throw them into a heap on the bed.

"Gemma, we've paid for some of the wedding and the invites have gone out."

I ignore him as I grab a suitcase from under the bed, fighting with it when it gets caught. "Were you with her last night?" He sighs again before nodding. "You prick. You made me think I was being unreasonable."

"I swear, I was gonna end it before we got married."

"Lies," I call out, throwing his clothes into the case. "Yah know what happened today?" When he doesn't respond, I laugh while tugging the zip closed. "A man kissed me."

"What?" He has the audacity to look pissed.

"I know, it's almost unbelievable that a man actually looked at me like I was the hottest thing in the room and then kissed me. And it was a good kiss," I rant, hauling the case from the bed and shoving it against his chest. "And I pictured him bending me over the desk and fucking me." I give a loud, crazy-sounding laugh. "And Christ, I wanted him too so badly. I wanted that feral sex I used to have before I met you." I shove him again. "But do you know what I did? I pushed him away. I told him to stay the hell away from me because I was getting married." I laugh again. "I'm a fucking idiot."

"This isn't like you," he mutters.

"It is," I yell. "It's exactly like me, but keeping hold of you was just another thing I was trying to do to please my fucking father. He said I wouldn't keep a good man like you." I groan out loud, throwing my head back. "A good man." I shake my head with a huff. "I really thought you were, but it turns out you're just like the rest. Now, get out, I never want to see you again."

# CHAPTER 5
### Fletch

I close my eyes and let my head fall back as London sucks my cock like a goddamn vacuum. "Jesus," hisses Nyx, moving faster. "We need to swap."

London releases me, and I growl in frustration, grabbing a handful of her hair and guiding her back to my erection. "I'll tell you when to stop," I snap.

Nyx grunts, shuddering through a release. "Fuck, man, I wanted to come in her mouth."

"Stop bitching. You're ruining my mood," I mutter, feeling the build-up of my own orgasm. I hold London's head, pushing my cock farther down her throat until I release, growling with each spurt.

I let go of her, and she coughs hard, digging her nails into my thigh. "What the fuck you gotta do that for?" she snaps, wiping her mouth on the back of her hand. "You don't gotta choke me, you dick."

Nyx laughs, moving over to the couch and grabbing his pack of cigarettes. London stomps out, not bothering to gather her clothes. "Moody bitch," I say, grabbing the sheet and pulling it over myself. "She's so uptight these days."

"Don't be falling to sleep on me," Nyx says, lighting his cigarette. "We're hitting the town."

"I'm knackered," I mutter. "You go without me. Have a good night."

"Brother, you've been a grumpy arsehole all week."

"I'm serious," I tell him. "I need some sleep."

---

I WAKE WITH A START. My mobile is vibrating across the bedside table, and I snatch it up, answering without checking the caller id.

"Brother," Nyx drawls.

"I told you, I ain't coming," I snap.

"You might change your mind when I tell you who I'm currently looking at," he pauses before adding, "your pig."

"Gemma?"

"Didn't you say she was getting married?"

"Yeah," I tell him, sitting up and reaching for the bedside light. I glance at my watch and see it's almost eleven.

"So far, she's stuck her tongue down three guys' throats. She ain't out here repping the married crew."

"Fuck," I mutter. "Send me your location. I'm on my way."

"No need, brother, we're in The Bar."

I disconnect, frowning. Is she looking for me? *Why else would she be there?*

I dress quickly and brush my teeth before heading downstairs. Lexi looks up from where she's lying on the couch. Luna is on the opposite one, and there are two empty bottles of wine on the table between them. "Where are you going?" they ask in unison then giggle.

"Business," I mutter, picking up the pace and heading out. The last thing I need is those two tagging along.

---

THE BAR IS PACKED out and I have to push my way through to get to the front where Grizz is serving. He glances up and grins when he spots me. "She's in a state," he tells me. "I had to stop serving her, and she ain't happy about it. I'd have kicked her out, but Nyx wanted to call you." He nods over to the far side of the room, where Gemma is hanging off some guy. It's clear she's drunk in the way she sways and grabs onto him to steady herself. "Thought this would be the perfect opportunity to start on that plan."

I watch as the man she's with places a finger under her chin and tips her head back slightly before kissing her. I roll my eyes as I push off the bar and head over. The man spots me first and breaks the kiss. "Can I help you?" He doesn't look impressed.

Gemma turns to see me and groans dramatically. "What are you doing here?"

"More like what the fuck are you doing here? Aren't you getting married?"

The guy takes a step back, and Gemma narrows her eyes. "Go away, Fletch. You don't know anything about my life."

She stomps out of the bar, shoving people as she goes, and breaks out into the fresh air. I'm right behind her as she takes a deep breath and practically stumbles. "Steady," I mutter, catching her, then she rightens and disentangles herself.

"What are you doing here?" she repeats, glaring at me.

"I don't know, Gemma, let me think," I say, my voice full of sarcasm. "Oh, yeah . . . my club owns this bar."

"I just came out for a quiet drink," she rants, "and here you are."

"Firstly, not quiet cos Grizz was ready to kick you out. Secondly, you've had your tongue down the throat of several men."

She gives me a triumphant look. "So, you've been spying on me."

"Ain't there some rules you coppers have to stick to? Are you even allowed in bars in this state?"

"I'm not in a state," she argues, swaying.

I arch my brow, and she leans against the wall. "I don't think you should be drinking in a place owned by people you wanna take down."

"Suddenly you care about my job?"

I shake my head. "Not even a little, but it's not like you to break the rules. What's going on, Snap?"

"Don't call me that," she mutters. She folds her arms over her chest and stares down at the ground. "I'm not that bad, am I?"

I sense the conversation is taking a serious tone, so I lean beside her against the wall. "Start at the beginning."

"Don't gloat," she warns before adding. "I'm not getting married."

"You lied?"

"Of course not," she snaps. "He's been cheating on me."

I allow the words to sink in. "Sorry to hear that, Snap."

"I don't snap," she says, irritation clear in her voice. "I'm the least snappy person ever."

I snicker. "Not how I remember yah."

"Well, anyway, I should go . . . home." The last word is spoken so sadly, it almost cracks my ice-cold heart.

"Will he be there?"

She shrugs. "I told him to get out, but he was never good at listening to me."

"Yah know, if you want, you could always come back to the clubhouse."

She scoffs. "Right, sure."

"I'm serious. If you need some time out, it's a good place to hide."

"I can't stay at the clubhouse," she mumbles, suddenly holding her hands to her stomach. "I feel sick," she adds, rushing over to the corner of the car park and vomiting onto the ground. I wince and follow, gently moving her hair from her face and rubbing her back.

"Stay one night, Snap. No one needs to know."

### Gemma

My head is spinning as Fletch lifts me off my feet and carries me over to the waiting vehicle. He gently places me in the back and fastens the seatbelt. "I'll meet you back at the clubhouse," he tells the driver before closing the door.

I allow my eyes to close and picture times when I felt happy . . . times with him. *Fletch*.

"Snap, wake up." I force my tired eyes open and stare into Fletch's. He smiles. "You need some water." Sliding his hand behind my head, he lifts me slightly, placing a glass of water to my lips. I take a sip, glancing around to find myself in a bedroom. "Don't panic, I'll sleep on the chair," he tells me, placing the glass on the side and laying me back on the soft pillows. I lift the sheets slightly to find myself in an unfamiliar T-shirt. "You were sick and you got some on your clothes," he says, noticing my frown. "I gave you one of my shirts."

"Who undressed me?" I ask, noting my voice is now raspy from the vomiting.

"I've seen it all before," he replies casually. "Besides, I didn't take off your underwear."

I roll my eyes and tuck the sheet under my chin. "I shouldn't be here."

"Don't overthink it."

"If my boss knew . . ."

"How will they find out?"

He's staring at me expectedly, like he wants me to confess to something. "If you're asking if I have this place watched, no . . . not yet."

"So, there's no way anyone can find out then." He settles back in the chair, getting himself comfy. "What are you gonna do now?"

"About?"

"Your boyfriend. Do you have a mortgage together, a dog?"

"He's my ex," I state, "and no to all of the above. I'm not that stupid to invest so much in someone only to get my heart ripped out all over again."

"A dig at me?"

I sigh but refuse to answer his questions. "I need to find uglier friends and a man who doesn't feel the need to fuck around behind my back." I push to sit up and fix him with a glare. "Is it me?" I demand to know. "Am I the problem?"

He shrugs. "I have no idea, Snap. I don't even know you these days."

"Back then . . . was it my fault back then when you shagged my best friend?" The words just tumble out like they've been there all along. Maybe they have. Since seeing him again, I've wanted to ask what I did wrong to make him do something so cruel. I don't even know why it bothers me so much, it was so long ago.

"Do we really need to drag up the past, Gem?" he asks, exasperated. "I don't even remember why I did what I did."

Disappointment sinks my stomach. Never having the answer means I can't truly close this door. "She's married now."

"I don't care."

"She's got a great life. Perfect."

Fletch sighs heavily. "Yah know one thing I've learned, Snap? Those who portray a perfect life are usually talking shit. No one's life is perfect." I've often thought the same. Kate is all smiles and fabricated chatter whenever I see her, not that I see her often as I avoid her at all costs. "How does it work, especially at Christmas time?" asks Fletch with a slight grin. "Like get-togethers with the family must be weird, right?"

"Pete's mum adores her, as they all do. She's the centre of attention whenever they're together. I, however, well . . . I'm just the deranged cop who lured poor Pete into a bad relationship." I scoff before adding, "If only they knew."

"So, why'd yah stay so long if it wasn't a happy relationship?"

I shrug. "Fear of the unknown . . . proving his family wrong . . . proving my father wrong . . ." I trail off, wondering why the hell I'm talking to Fletch about things I never really talk about at all.

He sits straighter. "So, everyone in his family and yours were waiting for your relationship to fail?"

"Pretty much."

"And you stuck it out because you wanted to prove a point?" He looks amused again.

"I don't like failure," I admit, picking at the material of the sheets.

"Sometimes things just have to fail so you can progress."

"Is that why we failed?" I ask, again wincing inside because I'm being way too open and forward.

He thinks over my question before pushing to stand and making his way over to the bed. He lowers carefully onto the edge and takes my hand. "I was a young lad, Snap. I thought with my dick . . . most of the time, I still do. I wish I could take back what I did, and you have every right to be pissed about it, but it was nothing you did. I was just a prick."

I bite my lower lip and lower my gaze. "I hate that I let you hurt me."

"I'm sorry," he says. "I am truly sorry."

"She laughed when I confronted her."

"Kate was a piece of work. She was always jealous of you."

"Did she pursue you?"

He sighs, dropping my hand. "Snap, you seriously want to go over all this, fourteen years on?"

"I need to," I admit. "Maybe what you did is setting up a pathway of destructive relationships because I . . ." I blink away tears. "I really loved you, and you broke my heart. I haven't been able to move past it."

When I raise my eyes to his, he looks guilty. "I've never had to face up to shit like this," he tells me, shifting until he's sitting beside me. "I'll be honest, Snap, I don't like it." He gives a small laugh. "Kate was easy. I was horny. It was as simple as that. She was there. It's a shit reason, but she made it clear she was interested, and I stupidly took the bait. She knew you were gonna turn up to hers, Gem. It was a setup."

"If I hadn't have turned up, I probably would never have known."

He gives a nod. "Maybe."

"You wouldn't have told me?"

He shrugs. "I don't know. Probably not. But we would have come to an end anyway."

"Why?"

"You were embarrassed of me."

I twist so I'm looking at him. "What?"

"We were hiding our relationship from your family, Gemma. We were sneaking around like what we were doing was bad."

"But you know what my father was like—he'd have ruined it."

"He ruined it anyway. Men like Pete are the ones women like you should be with. Your father would take one look at my tatts and arrest me." He adds a laugh, shaking his head. "Maybe I was hurt too. Maybe I did what I did so we'd just come to an end. I wasn't brave enough to just tell you. I couldn't deal with the fallout of it all and the hurt in your eyes. Turns out, I had to see that anyway."

"I wasn't ashamed."

"But you weren't proud either, and that made me feel like I was shit. Like I wasn't good enough, and God knows I'd had enough of feeling like that from everyone else."

"I'm sorry," I mutter, my brows pinching together. I'd never really thought about how he was feeling. "It wasn't intentional."

He gets up from the bed. "You need some sleep," he says, bending down to place a gentle kiss on my head.

I grab his hand before he can walk away. "I'm sorry," I say again. "I really am."

"It's all good, Snap," he says with a wink. "Sleep." And then he leaves the room.

# CHAPTER 6
**Fletch**

Axel looks up from his laptop when I knock on the office door. He indicates for me to step inside, which I do, closing the door behind me. "I brought Gemma back to the clubhouse," I inform him, and he narrows his eyes. "I saw it as an opportunity," I rush to add.

"Oh, please enlighten me on this bright idea," he mutters sarcastically.

"She was drunk, vulnerable. I thought it was the best time to pounce."

"Until tomorrow, when she wakes with a banging head and realises she spent the night in the club she's trying to take down."

The door swings open and Grizz stomps in. "Did you realise there's a copper in your bed?"

"He was just filling me in," says Axel, shaking his head in wonderment.

"Stay outta my room. And ain't there a saying about keeping your enemies close?" I ask. "Besides, I found out there's currently no surveillance on the club."

"Well, I assume not, seeing as she's here," says Grizz.

"Unless it's all a ploy," Axel points out.

"Nah, Pres, she's wasted. Besides, she broke up with her fiancé and is pretty cut up about it."

"Either way, having her here is a huge risk," he says.

"Having her here shows we have nothing to hide. I wouldn't just let her stay over if we were up to no good, right?"

"I've got a bad feeling this is all gonna go wrong," Axel admits.

"It won't," I reassure him. "I've got this. She's already opening up to me."

"Pres is right," Grizz agrees. "We didn't think it through. She could be up there right now, snooping."

"She's too drunk, and all she'll find is condoms and lube."

"If you're gonna make any headway, you should be up there fucking her brains out," says Axel.

"She's only just had her heart broken. I've gotta play this carefully."

"He's got a point," says Grizz. "Treating her like a friend would probably go down better."

"Whatever," Axel snaps. "Just don't bring her here and leave her alone. She's your responsibility."

I give a nod and head back up to the room to find Gemma sleeping peacefully. I smile, realising she still sleeps with her leg thrown over the sheets while hugging the pillow. I forgot how cute she looked like that.

I kick off my boots and strip to my boxers before lying down carefully beside her. Just being close to her might make me feel less guilty for what I'm about to do to her world once again. Hearing how upset she still is did nothing to ease the way I feel. I sigh heavily, placing my hands behind my head and staring up at the ceiling. She came for me first, that's how I have to look at it.

---

I INHALE, smelling vanilla, and slowly open my eyes. Gemma is snuggled against me with her leg thrown over mine, and I have my arms around her. She must sense I'm awake because she stirs too, stretching slightly before blinking her eyes a few times. I watch the confusion play out on her face, and when her eyes finally land on me, she gasps before unravelling from me and sliding over to the edge of the bed. "What the hell?"

I grin. "Don't pretend you're horrified, Snap."

"I just broke up with my fiancé."

I glance down at my morning hard-on and grin wider. "It might help you to feel better."

She eyes my erection and her cheeks flush red with embarrassment. "You're disgusting." I laugh, slipping my hand into my boxers. "What the fuck are you doing?" she gasps.

I close my eyes, shifting to get more comfortable as I wrap my hand around my thick cock. "What's it look like, Snap?"

"You can't do that in front of me," she hisses, pushing to stand. I smirk, running my eyes over the black lace underwear peeking out from under the shirt I leant her. And then she realises she's half-naked and tugs the shirt down.

"When did you become a prude?"

She glares indignantly. "I am not a prude. I just grew up."

I begin to move my hand slowly, keeping my eyes fixed on her. "And became a prude," I repeat. "You were so daring back then."

"Before I knew any better."

"You discovered you hated foreplay?"

Her cheeks burn a deeper red. "Where are my clothes?" she demands.

"In the wash."

"I can't leave here like this," she snaps.

"Then stay." I move my hand some more, and her eyes glance there before she spins around, turning her back to me. "Even better," I remark, checking out her backside again. "You got a good arse, Snap."

"Find me something to wear."

"Come on, Gem, relax. Let's have some fun."

"Seriously," she growls, then she marches for the door, ripping it open and stomping out the room.

I groan, diving off the bed and rushing after her. I catch her at the end of the hall. "Wait," I tell her, but she continues until I wrap my arms around her waist and press her against the nearest wall. "I'm sorry," I whisper. "I'll get you something to wear."

I feel her sag slightly, and then she turns in my arms and stares me in the eyes. "No more funny business," she warns.

I give a slight nod as my erection prods against her stomach. She arches a brow, and I smile. "Not my fault, you turned." I brush some stray hair from her cheek, and she gasps, her lips parting slightly. "Besides, you're so fucking beautiful, I can't help it."

A range of emotions passes over her face before she throws herself at me, taking me by surprise. She slides her arms around my neck and scrambles up my body until my hands grab her backside. I keep her against the wall, playing catch-up in my brain as her tongue explores my mouth. When I'm certain she's not going to change her mind, I carry her back to my bedroom and kick the door closed, not daring to break the kiss as I lower her to the bed.

### Gemma

I PUSH out the thousand doubts running through my mind as Fletch removes his shirt from me and runs kisses along my neck and over my chest. This could ruin everything I've worked hard for. Lord knows this would be enough for my father to have me kicked off the case.

I squeeze my eyes closed, allowing my mind to drift away and to lose myself in this moment. For once, I want to live in the moment.

Fletch pulls the cups of my bra down and stares for a second before taking my nipple in his mouth. A groan escapes me as he swirls his tongue over the swollen bud. He moves to the other, giving it the same delicious treatment. He slowly slides down my body, settling himself between my legs. Gently moving my knickers to one side, he wastes no time in swiping his tongue through my folds. Another groan escapes me. Peter hated giving me oral sex, and fuck, I've missed it. Fletch devours me, but it's not enough to drag an orgasm from me. I've always found it hard to let go unless I'm alone.

Fletch crawls back up my body, supporting himself on his arms as he stares down at me. "You gotta relax," he whispers, dropping a gentle kiss on my lips. Fletch was the first man to make me orgasm . . . and the last. Since him, no one's taken the time to bother. He taps my thigh and orders, "Roll over," and I do, because if I remember anything about Fletch, it's that he knows what he's doing. He slides a pillow under my hips and places one knee between my legs. I feel his hand there, rubbing his fingers through my juices before slipping one inside. "You ready, Snap?" he whispers, rubbing circles over my clit.

"Yes," I groan, burying my face in the sheets as he works his magic. He takes a fistful of my hair and tugs my head back.

I feel his breath at my ear. "You smell good," he growls, pushing another finger into me. I gasp as he moves them in and out, occasionally hooking them enough to hit that sweet spot. "I need to taste you some more," he continues. "Lift up, Snap."

I push onto all fours, and Fletch slides his face beneath me, hooking his arms around my thighs and tugging me down onto his waiting mouth. I shudder the second his tongue flicks my swollen bud. He pushes his fingers into me, moving them quickly, all the while licking and sucking. I come hard, my entire body vibrating with need.

I hear the faint sound of a packet ripping and then Fletch moves beneath me, sliding up my body. He smirks up at me, taking a handful of my hair again and pulling my mouth to his. I taste myself as he thrusts his tongue into my mouth.

His erection presses at my opening and he eases in, stretching me slowly, causing more sparks to ignite my nerve endings. Pushing me to sit upright, he unhooks my bra and stares at me with eyes full of lust. "Now, fuck me, Snap." I move, lifting off him and slamming down hard. He growls, cupping my breasts. "Again," he orders. I repeat the same action, and he closes his eyes. I move faster, lifting, dropping, lifting, dropping, until he grips my hips, stilling me. My breaths come in heavy bursts, and I know if he doesn't let me move soon, I might combust. I rock against him, and he releases my hips, allowing me to move freely. His thumb finds my clit and presses against it. I cry out, shuddering in surprise as I come apart for a second time. "My turn," he murmurs, spinning us until he's on top.

He pulls my hands until they're above my head, and he moves one of my legs up and over his shoulder before fucking me like a feral animal, thrusting so hard, I move up the bed. He comes on a roar, straining with his cock buried so far inside me, I feel it pulsing against my inner walls. "Fuckkk," he whispers, wiping the sweat from his forehead on the back of his arm. "Give me an hour, we're doing that again." And then he drops down beside me, breathing heavily.

---

I WAIT TWENTY MINUTES, until I'm certain Fletch is in a deep sleep, before slipping from his bed and creeping across to his walk-in wardrobe. I skim the rails of clothes, he always loved his designer shirts, and as I slip a black one from the rail, I notice it still has tags. I snap them off and pull it on. It's far too big, but what choice do I have? I can't be here when he wakes up, and we can't do that again. I find a belt and tie it around my waist to give the impression I'm wearing a shirtdress. When I go back into the bedroom, Fletch is wrapped in the sheets with his back to me, and I breathe a sigh of relief as I push my bare feet into my shoes.

I carefully open the door and slip out, rushing along the hall and down the stairs into the main room. I ignore the many bikers who are hanging around, but as I pass, I feel them looking my way.

"Officer?" The deep voice causes me to stop marching. I risk a quick glance as the club's president makes his way to where I am. "You okay?" I nod, turning my attention back to the exit and staring at it longingly. "Were you trying to sneak out of here?"

"No," I lie.

"You ashamed?"

"I just crashed for the night," I mutter, staring at the ground.

"You looked much more . . . confident last time you came by." I hear the smugness in his voice. He steps closer, and I fight the urge to step back. I won't back down from this man—I'm not scared. "I can smell the sex on you," he adds in a low whisper, and I clench my jaw in irritation. "Now, get the fuck outta my club. You're not welcome here."

I don't need to be asked twice, so I rush for the exit, sighing in relief when I break out into the fresh air.

---

I'M JUST out of the shower when there's a knock at the door. Still rubbing my hair with a towel, I pull it open to find my father there with Ruby. "You weren't picking up again," he spits, shoving Ruby into the house. She gives an eyeroll, and I smirk. She'd never do that to his face. "Your sister needs somewhere to stay for the rest of the week."

I frown. "How come?"

"Mum has one of her 'bad heads'," she retorts, using air quotes.

I fight another smile. "Okay, no problem." Sarah is ten years younger than my father, but she's been with him since I was eleven years old. I still refuse to refer to her as my stepmother, or even a relation at all. We've never seen eye-to-eye, and since Ruby came along, things have been so much worse between us.

Ruby goes off to dump her bag in the room I had decorated just for her. "Have you made any progress?" he asks, looking around the room with a disinterested expression.

"You mean with the Demons?" I shake my head. "Not yet."

"Don't get too close," he says, still not meeting my eyes.

"What are you talking about?"

"To him," he says, finally fixing me with a glare. "We don't need him coming back into our lives, into Ruby's life." And there it is, the real reason he doesn't want me to have anything to do with Fletch. "When Peter called to cancel dinner, he said you were working. Spending too much time on the case will give that biker the wrong idea."

"He's never been in her life," I say coldly. "We didn't give him a chance, remember?"

"And he never will be," he says firmly. "Make sure it stays that way." He heads for the door. "You know if he finds out the truth, he'll push his way into your life and hers. He's no good for you. He never was."

I remain in the doorway as he steps outside and turns back to me. "I didn't have to keep her," he reminds me. "I did that so you could still be a part of her life. I won't hesitate to put an end to that if you mess this up." He spins on his heel and stomps towards his car.

I slam the door and ball my fists. He's held Ruby over me far too many times, and I hate him for it. "You okay?" she asks from behind me, and I force a smile before turning to her.

"Yes, fine. How's school?"

She rolls her eyes and drops down on the couch. "Where's Perfect Peter?"

I smile at her name for Pete. "Why?"

"So I can avoid him."

I laugh. "Well, that won't be a problem from now on." I drop down beside her. "He's gone."

I feel her eyes burning into me as I reach for the television remote. "How come?"

I shrug, avoiding eye contact. "It just wasn't working."

"Thank fuck," she says, grinning.

I glare at her. "Language," I remind her, "and don't mention it to Father."

"Please, I'm almost fourteen. Kerry swears in front of her parents all the time and they don't even say anything. You're just my sister, relax." Her words sting, like they do every time she refers to me as her sister.

I tuck her hair behind her ear and cup her cheek. "You're so beautiful," I tell her, and she pulls away, making retching noises.

"You're so gross," she tells me, grabbing the remote. "Let's watch a horror."

# CHAPTER 7
### Fletch

"Any idea who tipped them off?" asks Grizz.

Axel shakes his head. "My man on the inside knows nothing."

"What about the copper? Did she scream out all her secrets while you fucked her?" Nyx asks.

"Nope. The only thing on her lips was my name," I say with a wink.

"Not fucking good enough," spits Axel. "Go find me something. I wanna know what they know."

"I told you, she's by the book, she'll never spill."

He narrows his eyes in annoyance. "Then you're not fucking her right. You need me to put someone else on it?" His words piss me off, and he smirks, knowing they've affected me. "Don't tell me you're feeling shit for her. We don't need that complication."

"Nah," I say quickly, "of course not. But she knows me. If she's gonna talk, it'll be to me."

He slams the gavel on the table and stands. "Glad we understand one another."

Atlas walks out with me. "What's the plan?" he asks.

I shrug. "I dunno. I don't think she'll risk her job."

"Brother, women do all kinds of stupid shit for love."

"Love?" I repeat.

"Yeah, you gotta make her fall for you if you want to break her."

I sigh. This keeps getting more and more complicated.

---

I WAIT across the road from the police station, by the old Scouts hut, and stare at my mobile phone. Gemma's reply comes instantly, and I grin.

> Snap: WTF. Stay there!!

I tuck my phone away and watch the gates slide open. Gemma rushes over the road towards me, and the second she's closer, she grabs my arm and drags me behind the Scouts hut. She shoves me hard against the wall, and I grin. "Easy, Snap."

"What the fuck are you doing here, Fletch?" she barks.

"I like it when you're in work mode," I reply, raising my hand to brush her hair from her face.

She slaps it away in annoyance. "I'm not messing. How dare you turn up here of all places?"

"You snuck out of my bed and then ignored my calls for the last two days."

"So, take a hint."

"Come on, Gem, don't act like we didn't have a good time."

"Is that why you're here," she hisses, "to fuck with my career?"

I grin. "You hurt me with your assumptions." I place a hand over my heart. "I'd never blackmail you."

She arches a brow. "Blackmail?" she repeats. "Are you shitting me? It's your word against mine."

"True." I begin to move away from her.

"What are you doing?"

"Seeing how much weight my word holds against yours."

She grabs me and hauls me back behind the wall. "Don't even think about it. I'll have you in a cell before you can even open your mouth."

"Is that a threat?" I ask, smirking.

"It's a promise," she snaps.

My smirk fades, and I grab her by the throat, pushing her against the wall. Her confusion gives me a second to take back control, and I turn her so she's facing away from me. I use my weight to keep her there and push my hand into her trousers. "Fletch," she mutters, but she makes no move to stop me as I push the material of her underwear to one side and brush my finger over her opening.

"Tell me to stop," I whisper close to her ear, and she closes her eyes. I rub faster as she turns her head slightly and her lips part. I kiss her, thrusting my tongue into her mouth, then I push two fingers into her and she parts her legs some more to give me access. It takes less than a minute before she comes hard, pressing both hands against the wall as she shudders uncontrollably.

I remove my hand and slide my fingers into my mouth to taste her. She watches, her cheeks pink from her orgasm and her lips swollen from our kiss. "Don't fucking threaten me again, Snap. It won't end well." I turn and walk away.

FLETCH

I GET BACK to the clubhouse to find most of my brothers out. I head into the kitchen and find Lexi and Luna helping Duchess. "What's going on?" I ask, resting against the worktop.

Axel enters the kitchen. "Just the person," he says, and I almost groan, wondering what joy I'm in for now. "Family dinner tonight. Bring the pig."

I frown. "Huh?"

He arches a brow in annoyance, and Lexi steps forward, placing a hand over his chest and tucking herself into his side. "What he means is, we're making dinner for tonight and we'd love for you to invite Gemma."

"Absolutely not." I can't think of anything worse.

"It wasn't a polite request," snaps Axel.

"Didn't you tell her she didn't belong in this club?" I remind him.

"Me and Grizz talked," he mutters. "We reckon if we keep her close, she'll crack."

"Pres, I'm already working on her, there's no need to make her feel welcome here." It's bad enough I'm gonna have to break her heart all over again without making her think we're one big, happy family.

"Bring her," he repeats before stomping out.

I roll my eyes, and Lexi catches me, smirking. "We're not that bad," she says. "Besides, what harm can it do?"

I pull my phone out and send Gemma a text.

> Me: You feel better after your midday release?

Her reply comes within seconds.

> Snap: Fuck off!
>
> Me: Temper, temper. Dinner tonight?
>
> Snap: I'd rather die.
>
> Me: Harsh. My President's invited you especially.

I wait for a good five minutes before her next reply comes.

> Snap: Okay. What time?
>
> Me: I'll come get you at seven.
>
> Snap: I'll walk.
>
> Me: Seven, Snap. Be ready.
>
> Me: And Snap, don't do anything stupid that would piss my President off . . . like come wired.

I head for Axel's office and find him staring into a glass of whiskey. He looks up. "I told her. She cleared it with her bosses."

"She told you that?" he asks, sounding surprised.

"Nope. She's at work and she took way too long answering when I told her you'd invited her."

"I kind of expected her to run it by them. She probably thinks she's gonna get something."

"What if she comes wired?"

He shrugs. "So, what if she does? I ain't planning on confessing my sins."

"I just think it's a little . . . dangerous."

"You're my Enforcer, Fletch, you love danger."

"What angle are we spinning here, Pres, just so we're all on the same page?"

"We need her to see there's nothing here for her. We're not some mastermind criminal gang."

"But we are."

He grins. "Does Lexi talk about club business?" I shake my head. "Because I hide it fucking well. If my own old lady doesn't know my business, that cop ain't gonna find shit out. She'll get bored and move on."

"So, that's the plan? Let her see there's nothing to hide and she'll get bored."

"The way I see it, she's gonna keep coming back uninvited if we don't become more open."

I shake my head. "She's not stupid, Pres. She'll know our plan."

"Just like we know hers. It's one big game that we can't afford to lose, so we're gonna do whatever we can to throw her off the scent."

I run my hands over my face, showing how exhausted I am. "So, who will be at this family dinner?"

"Just us, Grizz, and the women."

I give a nod. At least it's not the entire club. "I'm gonna get my head down for a few hours before I go get her."

## Gemma

## Nicola Jane

I RELEASE A LONG, nervous breath and brush my hair from my face. I don't know why the fuck I agreed to this dinner. That's a lie. I had no choice cos when I told my Chief Superintendent, she forced me to accept. We're not stupid —we know it's a show. The club's President probably thinks that by being open and welcoming, I'll assume they have nothing to hide, but with the intelligence we have on the club so far, there's no way we're falling for the clean-up act.

Ruby watches me from the couch. "Who is this guy?"

"Someone I used to know. No one important."

There's a loud knock at the door, and I jump in fright. *Fuck, why am I so nervous?* Ruby dives up from the couch and rushes to open it, despite my protests. She returns seconds later with a huge grin on her face and Fletch standing behind her.

"He's got tatts," she states, arching a judgmental brow. "What will our father say?" And then she laughs, knowing full well what he'd say.

"You're early," I say, glancing at my watch and noting it's only quarter-to.

"I knew you'd leave before I got here," he replies, and I almost smile because he's right. I was just about to leave to avoid seeing him here in my home, with Ruby just a few steps away. I stare at the pair, noting how similar they look, and my heart squeezes.

"Anyway, we should go," I say, grabbing my bag.

"Hold on," he says. "Aren't you going to introduce us?"

I glance at Ruby, who looks amused by my flustered state. "Ruby, this is Fletch. Fletch, this is my younger sister, Ruby."

He smiles wide, and she holds out her hand. They shake, and he arches a brow. "Good handshake. Strong."

"Gem taught me to look a man in the eye and shake hard," she replies.

He looks impressed. "How old are you, Ruby?"

"We really should go," I cut in. "Ruby, lock the door behind us."

"Why don't you come?" asks Fletch, and I freeze.

"No, that's not a good idea," I say, now trying to bustle him towards the exit.

"Snap," he says firmly, and I still, "what's gotten into you? Ruby, there's plenty of food if you want to come."

"And play third wheel? No, thanks."

"It's not a date," I say, glaring back at her.

"She's right," Fletch agrees. "It's a work thing, right, Gem?" The way he stares at me, challenging me to deny it, makes my skin prickle.

"Right," I confirm, and he looks away, an annoyed expression on his face. "Besides, Father would have a fit if I took you along," I tell Ruby.

"God forbid," mutters Fletch as he heads for the door. Ruby gives me a little wave, and I follow Fletch.

By the time we arrive at the clubhouse ten minutes later, I'm fully nervous. I don't usually get like this, but being this close to Fletch changes things.

I follow him inside and am surprised to see no one in the main room. He leads me towards the kitchen, stopping right outside the door and turning to me. "I need to check," he mutters, looking uncomfortable.

"For?" I know exactly what he means. He wants to see if I'm wired-up. I roll my eyes and lift my shirt. Fletch takes the hem and lifts it higher, then he runs his hands around my back, gently stroking my skin before dropping onto his haunches and feeling up my legs. "Seriously," I say, "I'm not wearing anything." He gives a satisfied nod and stands.

He pushes the door open and the smell of food hits us, making my stomach growl in hunger. The sound of laughter and chatter makes me smile, as it's not something I've ever really experienced. When I lived at home, we had to eat at the table in silence, and with Pete, well, we never really laughed and we never really sat down to eat together.

Axel is sitting at the head of the table, and Lexi is on his knee with her arms around his neck. Luna is standing with her child in her arms while Grizz is telling them some tale that has them all engrossed, until we step farther into the room and everyone falls silent. I give an awkward smile, but no one returns it. Luna is the first to speak, announcing that she needs to put the baby to bed, and she passes us without another word.

Axel stands, placing Lexi on her feet beside him. "Welcome to my club," he says. "Take a seat." He points to the one beside him and then half pulls it out. Lexi moves to his other side and sits, so I do the same. Fletch sits beside me, shrugging from his kutte and placing it on the back of his chair.

"It smells amazing, Lex. What we got?" he asks.

"Luna made bread," she announces, pointing to the fresh loaf in the centre of the table. "And I made chicken pie." She proceeds to lift the lids on the pots in the centre of the table. "I hope you're not a veggie," she adds, looking at me, and I shake my head.

Everyone begins to help themselves to the food. Fletch

fills my plate as Luna returns minus the child. "You never said you had a sister," Fletch remarks. The others are making conversation amongst themselves, so I welcome the attention, even if it is about a subject I'd rather avoid with him.

"She's my half-sister."

"I gathered," he says. "She looks like you."

"We're close."

"How old is she?"

"Thirteen."

"I didn't realise your father was the Chief of Police" Axel says, finally bringing his attention to me. The rest of the group stops talking and looks my way.

I sit straighter. "Yep."

"I've met him a few times."

"He likes to get to know the locals."

"Is that how you got so far up in the force?" asks Lexi, and I narrow my eyes on her. I expect those assumptions from men, as I get them all the time, but women usually know how hard we have to work to prove we can do the same job as the men.

"No," I say firmly, "I moved away and worked hard. I only came back here recently."

Fletch grabs the whiskey decanter and pours two glasses, sliding one nearer to me and taking his own. "She never wanted to be a copper, did you?" he asks and looks at me.

"I don't remember," I reply.

"You do," he persists. "You wanted to grow flowers and sell them in your own shop."

"I love flowers," says Luna, and she gives me a small smile.

"So, what happened?" asks Grizz.

I shrug. "I just changed my mind."

"Bullshit," mutters Fletch, and I glare at him. "Your father forced you to join the police."

"My father didn't want me to join, actually," I correct him. "In fact, he was pissed when I transferred over."

"You joined to prove him wrong," says Lexi thoughtfully.

"And taking us down would really make him see your worth," adds Axel.

I shift uncomfortably. "It's just my job," I say.

"Bull. You want this club for a reason, but I get it, you're playing your cards close to your chest," says Axel. "We're running legit these days."

"Is that why you invited me here and had your Enforcer check me for wires?" I ask, arching a brow. I note how Axel gives Fletch a look that says he's not happy. "Whoops," I whisper. "Did he break command . . . go rogue?"

Axel's lip lifts slightly. "Maybe Fletch just wanted to cop a feel. I hear you two are getting close these days."

I feel my cheeks redden slightly, but I refuse to match his childish digs. "Or maybe he was checking me for wires," I repeat more firmly.

"I don't like the idea of you coming into my family to set us up," says Fletch. "Pres is right, we're running legit, but I know what your lot are like. And this is a private dinner. We don't need your mates listening in."

We spend a few minutes eating in silence when Luna clears her throat, making us all look in her direction. "You shouldn't give up on your dreams," she announces, staring at me. I frown, and she smiles. "If you want to make floral arrangements, you should. You're not at work all the time, right? I made bread on the side before I had Ivy."

I force a smile, trying to recall her file. "What did you do?" I ask, mainly to be polite because I remember that she worked in the slut house for the club.

"I was a sex worker," she says almost proudly, and I want to roll my eyes. "But now, I make bread at Grizz's bar."

"Really? What made you give up your job?" It's a normal question you could ask anyone, except for here in a biker club. I try not to smirk.

"I never wanted to work in the sex industry, obviously," she says with a small laugh. Grizz places a hand over hers and gives a slight shake of his head. Luna narrows her eyes. "She asked a question, I answered."

"Nothing to hide, huh?" I repeat, arching a brow in Axel's direction. It's clear the women aren't allowed to speak to me.

"My mum was a shit mum," Luna continues, pulling her hand free of Grizz's. "She was an addict. I don't know if you know much about addiction, but it consumed her life . . . and ours."

"You have siblings?" I ask, again to be polite because her prick of a brother has been missing for months and I suspect that's something to do with this club.

"Just me and my brother."

I take a bite from a chunk of bread and almost roll my eyes in delight. It's like a fluffy piece of heaven. "Do you get along?"

"No. In fact, I haven't seen him for a while," she says, glancing at Grizz, who's gripping his cutlery extra hard by the looks of his white knuckles.

"Really?" I ask. "What about you, Grizz? Have you seen him?"

"You got something to ask me?" he spits.

I shake my head. "Nope. Just wondering."

"Anyway," Luna continues, "I was forced into sex work as a kid by my father . . . and then my brother."

I glance down at my plate, wondering what sort of parents would do that. "Sorry to hear that."

"And once you're in that life, it's hard to get out."

"Especially when her brother pimped her out," snaps Grizz.

"He should face charges for that," I tell him. "Have you put in a complaint against him?" I ask Luna.

"No. No offence, but he had my baby taken from me. I'm not going to make a complaint and have him back here, only for you guys to let him go. That's what usually happens," she says, "I don't exactly have trust in the police or the justice system."

"Wine anyone?" asks Lexi, standing to grab a bottle from the side. She proceeds to fill three wine glasses without waiting for a response, placing one in front of me, then Luna, and downing the last one herself.

"Let's cut the crap," I say, and she almost chokes on the last gulp. "You want me to embrace the welcome, accept you're all legit, and leave you alone."

"We just want to be treated fairly," says Axel. "Dawn raids when we have kids here—"

"One kid," I correct.

"It's unsettling," he snaps.

"For the baby or you?"

"What do you expect to find?" he shouts.

"Everything you're doing wrong," I tell him, pushing

my chair back from the table. "I'm not blind, Axel. I see that this club runs this area, and it's time that stopped. You don't own these streets, and it's not your job to police them the way you see fit. You can't off pimps on a whim or chase off new dealers so you can supply the addicts." I throw my napkin on the table and stand. "So, if I have to keep dropping in those dawn raids to disrupt your daily dealings, then I will."

# CHAPTER 8

### Fletch

I let out a long sigh as Gemma storms from the kitchen. Axel rolls his eyes. "Go after her," he orders.

"And say what?" I hiss, "I told you this was a bad idea."

He fixes me with a glare that tells me he's about to erupt, so I sigh again for dramatic effect and go after her.

She's almost at the gate when I catch up and grab her arm to slow her down. "Not so fast," I say with a laugh. "Why are you so mad?"

"Because this shitshow was a setup," she yells, turning on me. "I am a fucking police officer, Fletch. I lock people like you up, and here I am, sitting at a table with you and your boss."

"He's not my boss," I mutter.

"Whatever he is," she screams, waving her arms in the air. "And they're all questioning my motives like they have no idea what I am or who I am."

I take her hand and tug her a step closer. "I remember who you were before this," I say, tucking her hair behind her ear. "And tonight, I just wanted to see her again."

"Why?" she demands.

"Because I liked her."

"I'm not that girl anymore, Fletch," she snaps. "You saw to that."

"Then maybe I need to get to know who you are now."

"Why?"

"Because . . ." I groan, "maybe I just want to."

"It's not enough," she mutters, going to turn away, but I keep hold of her. "Fletch, this can't happen between us."

"What can't?"

"This," she hisses, waving a hand between us, "whatever this is, just stay away from me."

"I can't," I blurt. The panic that she's trying to walk away for good, and how Axel will react to that, makes me pull her back to me. "I can't," I repeat, cupping her cheek and placing a gentle kiss to her lips.

"I'm gonna take down your club."

I give a slight nod, pressing my forehead against hers. "I know. We survived for two years living in secret."

She laughs. "You're kidding, right?"

I shake my head and kiss her again. "There's nothing wrong with two adults hooking up."

"Hooking up?" she repeats.

"We're both single, consenting adults."

"Only I'm a police officer and you're a criminal."

I grin. "You have no evidence to back that, officer."

She begins to pull away again. "I can't."

"At least until you have something on us," I try. "What happened to innocent until proven guilty?" She begins to walk, and I follow her out the gate. "Come for a drink with me," I add, giving puppy dog eyes for added effect, and a smile pulls at her lips.

I guide her to the nearest bar, and we sit in a dark corner away from everyone else, nursing two whiskeys. "I feel like we've reached an understanding," I tell her, and she rolls her eyes. "Hear me out. We're actually talking now, so that's a start, isn't it?"

"My father would have a shitfit if he saw us together," she mutters.

"He still a wanker?"

"He's certainly taking 'grumpy old man' to the next level."

"What's he think about your breakup?"

"I haven't told him, but no doubt Pete will fill him in the second he gets a chance."

"You don't seem very upset over it," I remark, and she stares down into her drink.

"We were never going to work," she admits. "He's a stuck-up prick with more money than sense." She sighs. "He got me a new car."

I raise my brows in surprise. "A nice one?"

She grins. "A beamer."

I laugh. "Makes sense."

"He wanted to change me."

"How?"

She shrugs. "To be the perfect wife. He wanted me to hold dinner parties and entertain his boring surgical associates. We never did anything fun together."

"He sounds like a dream."

"He was a carbon copy of my father, and I have no fucking clue why I ever went for him because I hate my father." Her admission means she's opening up and relaxing.

"You always felt a need to keep him happy."

She nods in agreement. "Fat lot of good that did me."

"And he went on to have another kid," I say, my words sounding every bit surprised.

"Ruby isn't keen on him either," she tells me. "I wish I could get her away from him."

"He's her father, and I'm sure her mother makes up for the parts he's lacking."

Gemma scoffs. "She's a witch."

"It's surprising anyone puts up with your father, so hats off to her."

Gemma rolls her eyes again, "She sticks around because of what he gave her." She shakes her head, frowning slightly. "I mean, what he can give her."

"A money grabber?"

"Sort of. Tell me about you," she says, sipping her drink. "Not club life, just . . . life."

"Not much to tell."

"You used to say that a lot, Fletch. But what about your childhood and your parents? What happened to them?"

"I'm a lone wolf," I say with a grin, finishing off my drink. "Another?" I ask, tipping my empty glass to her. She nods, and I head back to the bar.

---

I INSTRUCTED the bartender to keep the drinks flowing, and after three more double whiskeys for Gemma and only single pours for me, she's a lot more relaxed. Her cheeks have a healthy glow, and she's laughing at all my crap jokes.

"I shouldn't have drunk so much," she mumbles, narrowing her eyes when the bartender places another two drinks at the end of the bar. I take them, handing her one.

"You're allowed to drink when you have a broken heart," I say, winking.

"What's your excuse?" she asks with a smirk.

"I'm your moral support."

She laughs. "Morals? You don't have any of those."

I press my hand to my chest and fake hurt. "I've grown up."

"Bullshit. When was your last serious relationship?" I bite my lower lip, trying hard to hide the smirk. "Exactly," she states, laughing harder. "If I had a mother, she'd have told me to stay away from guys like you."

"Would you have listened?"

It's her turn to chew on her lip, and she gives her head a shake. "It's easy to get lost when I'm with you," she admits, not quite meeting my eyes.

I drain my drink. "Maybe you're not lost, Snap. Maybe you're exactly where you're supposed to be." I place my glass down and move her full one from her reach. "Let's get you home."

"Home?" she repeats, almost looking confused.

"Yep, that place you lay your head at night," I tease, standing and holding out my hand. She eventually takes it and allows me to tug her to stand. She falls against my chest, and when she raises her head and her eyes meet mine, there's heat there. She glances at my lips, her tongue darting out to wet her own. "You want me to kiss you, Snap?" I whisper, brushing her hair away from her face and gently cupping her cheek. "In public?"

"You didn't used to be shy," she murmurs. I press my lips to hers, softly placing a kiss there. Her hands circle my neck and she presses herself against me to deepen the kiss. When we pull apart, she's panting breathlessly. "Bathroom," she says, arching a brow as if she's challenging me. Then she steps away, heading for the ladies' bathroom.

I stay rooted to the spot, glancing around casually while weighing up my options. It takes me less than a second to follow.

I shove the door open, and she spins to face me, leaning against the condom machine and holding her hands behind her back like a child being caught stealing. I close the gap between us and push my fingers into her hair, pulling her to me and taking control of her mouth again. I reach behind her and retrieve the condom before walking her backwards into the nearest cubicle. It's a tight squeeze, and while I unfasten my jeans, I lower onto the closed toilet seat. It breaks the kiss, so Gemma reaches under her dress and shimmies from her underwear. I rip open the condom and pull out my erection. She eyes me lustfully, watching as I roll the rubber over my length, and then she throws a leg over me and lowers onto me, groaning the second my cock slides into her tightness. I squeeze my eyes closed for a second, enjoying the feel of her choking me. She holds onto my shoulders, lifting herself and slamming down hard. "Fuck," I hiss, squeezing her hips. "Slow down."

"I need this," she pants, moving faster.

She leans back slightly, placing her hands on my knees and giving me access to her clit. I gather some of her wetness on my thumb and press it against her swollen bud. She groans. "Oh shit," she whispers, closing her eyes. A blush creeps up her neck and over her cheeks as her swollen lips part, letting out small gasps of pleasure as her orgasm washes over her.

I lift her and press her against the closed door. "You're addictive," I murmur, squeezing her backside. I fuck her hard, not bothering that the door is banging with each thrust. And when I finally come minutes later, a low growl escapes from the back of my throat as I strain, pushing in as far as she can take me.

I still, pressing my head against her shoulder while I catch my breath. I lower her feet onto the ground, and she wipes my brow with her hand. "We should do that again back at mine," she whispers with a giggle. I'm not about to refuse, so I grab a handful of tissue, remove the condom, and drop it in the waste bin. Then I fasten my jeans while she slips her underwear back in place and straightens her tousled hair. I take her by the hand, and we step out to find a woman waiting patiently. She stares at the ground as we pass, giggling like naughty teenagers.

We walk hand-in-hand back to Gemma's place. She doesn't seem to care we're out in public or that we could be seen, and I don't waste my breath reminding her because I like it when she's like this, so calm and relaxed.

The lights are out, and she carefully unlocks the door, allowing us to slip in quietly. She locks it behind us, throwing her keys on the side before taking me by the hand again and leading me upstairs.

The second we're in her bedroom, I wrap my arms around her and kiss her. It's going to be a long night.

## Gemma

"WHAT THE FUCK!"

My eyes shoot open, and Pete is staring at me from the bedroom doorway. I blink a few times, squinting as light peeks through the curtains. "Pete," I croak, realising my throat is dry.

"Who the fuck is he?"

I glance to my left and gasp in horror as Fletch stirs, stretching out and causing the sheet to fall away from his naked body. I sit up, groaning as my head spins. "Shit," I mutter, covering my face as my mind replays last night. "Shit, shit, shit."

"Answer me," Pete yells.

Fletch groans aloud. "Shut him up, my head's banging."

"Is this a joke?" Pete demands, glaring at me.

I scrub my hands over my face. "Go downstairs, I'll be there in a second."

"Or we could do it now," he shouts, closing the gap between us and ripping the sheet from me. I screech, trying desperately to grab it back, but when he sees I'm naked too, a painful cry leaves him. I jump up, making a grab for him to comfort or soothe his pain, but he jumps back, looking at me in disgust. "Don't fucking touch me, you slag."

His words hurt, and I drop back onto the bed and frown. "Pete," I whisper.

"Is this why you kicked me out? So this . . . this . . . *criminal* can jump in your bed?"

"No," I begin to protest.

"Who said I'm a criminal?" asks Fletch, pushing to sit up. He grabs his T-shirt from the floor and pulls it over my head. If it wasn't for the utter panic I'm currently feeling,

I'd think it was sweet he'd taken the time to cover me up. "You're purely seeing the tatts and jumping to assumptions. Not cool, man."

"Fuck you," Pete hisses angrily.

Fletch arches a brow as he pulls on his boxer shorts. "You're being a prick."

"You're fucking my wife!" Pete screams.

Fletch stands, and I groan. "Firstly, she ain't your wife. Secondly, she kicked your cheating arse out for good reason."

"She told you?" asks Pete, sounding astounded. He brings his hateful glare back to me. "How long has this been going on?"

"Nothing's going on," I mutter feebly.

"You told him about our private business, Gem. Who the fuck is this wanker?"

"We'll have less of the name calling," snaps Fletch.

"Get out," Pete demands. "Get out of here and stay the hell away from my wife."

"Again, she's not your wife."

"Fletch," I hiss, "just go."

"Me go?" he snaps.

"You heard her, get out," Pete adds, then his eyes narrow. "Hold on . . . Fletch?" He glances at me then back at Fletch. "Not Cameron Fletcher?"

Fletch grins. "The one and only."

"Please, just give us a moment. I need to talk to him," I mutter, risking a glance in Fletch's direction. He begins to dress, and when I go to remove his shirt, he shakes his head, grabbing his kutte and storming out. *Great.*

"What the hell is he doing back?" Pete hisses.

"It doesn't matter."

"It fucking matters," he yells.

"Can you stop yelling?" I growl. "Ruby is here."

"Oh wow," he grumbles, shaking his head and placing his hands on his hips. "So, you had a criminal here to fuck while your little sister was stopping over?"

"Why are you even here?"

"To sort things out, but I don't know if I want to after seeing you with him."

I scoff. "Are you actually serious? After everything you've done?"

He sighs, running a hand through his hair. "You're right," he states, his hand dropping to his side. He perches on the edge of the bed. "You're right. Let's call it quits."

I laugh, waiting for him to tell me he's joking. When he doesn't join me, my smile fades. "You're being serious?"

He grabs my hand. "Babe, this can work. We just need to talk things through and be honest with one another."

"Honest?"

"Yes. If I can just explain what I find in those women that I don't find in you, maybe we can work through it."

I pull my hand away, his words twisting at my heart. "Like what?"

He takes a breath like he's preparing some speech, and I brace myself. "For starters, your underwear could do with an update." My brows must reach my hairline because he rushes to add, "You've had some of them since we met."

"What else?" I demand, moving on swiftly.

"We could try some new stuff?"

"In the bedroom?"

"Yeah, yah know, like some kinky stuff."

"You'd need to be a little more specific," I hiss as calmly as I can muster.

"I like to be . . . well, I want you to tie me up."

"Tie *you* up," I repeat slowly.

"And maybe hit me sometimes."

"Hit you?" I'm struggling to hide the shock displaying clearly on my face.

He suddenly looks unsure. "I get off on pain." I have no words, so I stare at him open-mouthed. "And being dominated," he adds, staring down at his knotted fingers.

"Oh god," I murmur.

"And if you agree, I'd like you to meet Alice."

"Alice?" I almost whisper while trying to fight the vomit that wants to make an appearance.

"She's on board with the whole idea," he gushes enthusiastically.

A small, unamused laugh escapes. "Maybe you could run it by me, Pete, cos I'm not sure I am."

"The three of us."

My brows arch again. "Together?"

He nods, smiling. "You both dominating me."

I pinch the bridge of my nose, letting his confessions sink in. "Why didn't you ever tell me any of this?"

"Because I was ashamed," he admits, "but after I spoke with Alice, she convinced me to talk to you. She thought you'd be a little more understanding about why I tend to stray."

"Oh, did she?" I mumble, releasing a sigh. "Look, this isn't going to work."

He grabs my hand again. "Gemma, it is. You just need to try it . . . for me."

I pull free and stand, heading over to the window. "And what about me? What about what I want?"

"You want me," he tells me. "We can still get married and be the happy couple your father expects."

I scrub my hands over my face. "No," I state clearly. "I've spent my entire life trying to please everyone but me, and I'm not doing it anymore. I'm glad you found the courage to tell me how you feel because, honestly, I really thought it was me. Now, I see it's just a difference in what we want."

"Gemma, just think about it. We can be happy."

"As long as I give you what you want," I say, spinning to face him. "I don't want to dominate a man. In fact, I want a man who can dominate me. A man who can throw me around the bedroom like a rodeo cowboy. I want a man who takes care of me before himself." He looks offended. "I want a man who can make me come."

"I can make you come," he snaps.

"Never," I yell, throwing my hands in the air. "Not one time. I faked it."

"How the hell am I supposed to make you come when I think you already have?"

"Because you don't do it for me, Pete," I say, exasperated from the lies I've been telling us both since we began dating. "And now, I know why. Because I don't do it for you either."

"But he does?" he spits. "What would your father say, seeing you with a man like that?"

I laugh. "He'd hate it, but I'm a grown adult and I can do what I want. I'm calling the wedding off. In fact, I'll start calling people today and cancelling everything."

"You're making a mistake," he says, heading for the

door. "And don't think you can come crawling back when you realise it."

---

I RING my father's doorbell. His house is grand, with lavish stone carvings adorning the brick wall surrounding the property. The door is always locked, but I've never had the pleasure of being given a key, and neither has Ruby, who waits patiently beside me.

When he finally opens the door, he frowns at the pair of us. "I didn't call."

"I know," I say, stepping forward so he has no choice but to open the door wider and let us in. I dump Ruby's overnight bag in the hall and head on through to the kitchen, where Jolene, his housekeeper, is baking. When she spots me, she smiles wide and holds out her floured hands for a hug. I go to her immediately, comforted by the smell of her lavender perfume. It's the same perfume she's worn since I was a small child. "How are you, my gorgeous girl?" she asks.

"I'm good. What are you making?"

She moves to hug Ruby. "Bread," she announces proudly. "I haven't quite perfected it." She senses my father coming and goes back to kneading her dough.

"I've made dinner plans for this evening," he says coldly.

"Where's Sarah?"

"I told you, she isn't well."

"Still?" He hates questions, and he sighs like I'm annoying him. "I have a shift tomorrow and things to do," I explain. "And Ruby is bored at mine." Ruby kisses me on the cheek and goes out of the room. "Besides," I add, "I need to talk to you."

"Fine," he mutters, turning and heading for his office. I follow, closing the door behind me. He sits in his oversized chair and fixes me with his narrowed, angry eyes.

"Peter and I have split up."

My father sits straighter. "I'm sorry, what?"

"It wasn't working out."

"You're getting married."

"Not anymore."

He slams his hands on the table and rises to his feet. "You *are* getting married," he declares, each word firmer than the last.

"Why do you care?"

"I have invested a lot of money into Peter and his practice."

"So?"

"I thought he was going to be a part of the family."

"Shit happens," I mutter.

"This better not have anything to do with that club," he hisses, his voice low and dangerous.

"Why would my relationship have anything to do with The Chaos Demons?"

"You tell me?"

"Pete was cheating on me," I blurt.

"So?"

"What do you mean, so? He was having sex with another woman behind my back. I can't marry him."

"Of course, you can. Men have needs. It doesn't harm the marriage to occasionally experiment."

"Oh my god," I mutter in disgust. "I haven't come here to discuss it with you. I've come here to tell you the wedding is off, so if you've invited people, you should tell them."

"I can't call the MP and tell him the wedding I've paid thousands towards is cancelled," he snaps.

"You've paid towards? I've not asked you for a penny." He glances away, and I sigh heavily. "Pete asked you?"

"It doesn't matter. I will not call my guests to cancel."

"Then don't," I hiss, heading for the door, "but they'll need an explanation when they attend a wedding with no fucking bride or groom."

# CHAPTER 9
**Fletch**

Every brother has his eyes fixed on me. "It went well, but she didn't give up any information," I explain with a shrug.

"She kicked you out when her ex turned up," says Grizz with a laugh, and I instantly regret filling him and Axel in before church.

"But she relaxed around me, that's the main thing."

"We need something on her," Axel says, and Grizz nods in agreement.

"Like what? I told you, she's by the book."

"A sex tape?" he suggests.

I laugh. "Are you joking?"

"Do I look like I'm fucking joking?" he snaps. "A threesome?"

"Not a chance," I snap.

"Did I fucking stutter? Are you choosing this bitch over the club?" He glares, daring me to give him the wrong answer.

"Pres, ain't it an offence to film her without her consent? Besides, I don't think she's into threesomes."

"Then convince her," says Grizz with a smirk. "Nyx, you're usually up for that kind of shit."

I glance over at Nyx, who's staring at me with the same uncertainty I'm feeling. "Sure, VP, whatever," he mutters.

"We can use that to keep her in line," adds Axel.

The knot in the pit of my stomach is growing by the hour, and I suddenly feel sick. I've already hurt her deeply, and now, I'm going to do it all over again. "She might've worked shit out with her ex," I say, and I can't help the feeling of hope at that thought.

"Then get round there and make a scene. Do whatever you have to do to win her back," says Axel.

I give a nod, even though my heart isn't in it. Usually, I'd be up for this sort of shit, anything to protect my club and my brothers, but something about what we're doing to Gemma feels wrong, and it ain't often I get a conscience.

---

I KNOCK LOUDLY, and a second later, Gemma practically rips the door open. She scowls. "What are you doing here?"

"I just came to check on you, but if you're gonna be a bitch about it . . ." I turn and head back down the garden path.

"Wait," she snaps, and I slow, hiding the smile as I turn to face her. "I'm fine. I called in sick to work," she admits, heading inside and leaving the door open for me to follow.

Inside, she's filling the kettle, and I take a seat at the breakfast bar. "Nice place," I remark, looking around the large kitchen. "Are you sick?" I ask.

"No, I'm tired and pissed-off."

"Because of me?"

She shakes her head. "No. I spent the entire day on the telephone cancelling my wedding. I've lost thousands."

"You didn't sort it out with perfect Pete?" A part of me feels relieved until I remember what I have to do.

"Nope. He ended up explaining why he isn't happy, and I couldn't see a way forward."

"Sounds intriguing."

She half smiles, turning the kettle off before it's boiled. "If I'm going to tell you about that, I need a real drink." She reaches into a cupboard and retrieves a bottle of scotch. It's not my tipple, but I don't argue as she pours us each a glass and hands me one.

She heads out the room, and I follow her into the living room, which is perfect with not a thing out of place. "I hate this room," she explains, grabbing a pile of magazines and spreading them across the shelf. "It had to be tidy all the time."

I smirk at the pile of magazines. "And that's your way of rebelling?"

She laughs and grabs some cushions from the large sofa, dropping them on the floor, then she laughs again. "I'm going to leave them there overnight."

"Rebel," I tease.

We sit, and she takes a sip of her drink. "He wanted more kink."

I grin. "And you didn't?" My heart thuds harder. How the fuck can I convince her into a threesome if she doesn't even like a bit of kink?

"Oh, I have no problem with it, but not when he wants me to control the whip. No, thanks."

I relax at this information. "I think you'd suit a Dominatrix situation," I say with a grin.

"And then he insisted we still marry and take part in some kind of threesome with his mistress."

I arch a surprised brow. "Wow."

"Exactly."

"You're not into the threesome scene?" I ask carefully.

"Are you?" she asks.

I shrug. "I don't mind it if everyone is consenting."

She sits straighter. "You've done it?" I nod. "With another man and woman or two women?"

"Both."

She rolls her eyes. "Of course, you have."

"Haven't you ever wondered what it would be like to have two men worshipping you?"

Her cheeks pink as she stares down into her glass. "No."

"Liar," I say with a smirk. "I get why you wouldn't want to dominate him, though."

She looks up. "You do?"

"You want to be taken care of. Under all that strong female energy you got going on, you want a man to take control in the bedroom." She visibly swallows. "So, having two men take control of you can be exhilarating."

"I'll take your word for it." She knocks her drink back in one.

"You wanna get some food?" I ask.

She smirks. "Are you asking me on a date?"

"Nope, that would be wrong seeing as you're on the rebound. But I'm hungry, and you're gonna get shitfaced again. You can't do that on an empty stomach."

"I called in sick," she mutters. "I might get seen."

"I'll take you somewhere the police never go."

She bites her lower lip while she considers it, then she jumps up. "Let me get ready."

She returns twenty minutes later in jeans and a vest top. She stuffs her feet into heels and grabs a handbag off the side. "Let's go."

Ten minutes later, I slow the bike outside The Bar, and we get off. Gemma straightens her hair as I put her helmet away. "I'm getting better on that contraption," she tells me.

I grab her hand and lead her inside. It's not too busy and we manage to get a table. I head to the bar, where Grizz is watching her as she takes a seat. "Two whiskeys. Make hers double," I say.

He grins. "Is that how you get her to sleep with you?"

"Do you want me to get the tape or not?"

He pours two drinks. "You like her," he states. I ignore him, and he adds, "You look at her the way you used to look at Luna." We don't talk about the fact I liked his old lady when he was still trying to push her away.

"She's an ex. There's history, but it's nothing."

"If you think this could go somewhere, just say the words and Pres will come up with another plan."

I shake my head and take both drinks. "The club is my priority," I tell him, heading back to Gemma.

"He doesn't like me," says Gemma, taking her drink as I sit down opposite her. I glance back at Grizz, who's still watching us while he wipes glasses.

"He doesn't like anyone."

"Except her," she says, nodding towards Luna.

I smile. "Everyone loves Luna. She's an angel sent to save our arses."

Gemma eyes me for a second before saying, "You love her."

I frown, shaking my head and taking a large gulp of my drink. "Don't be ridiculous. She's with my VP."

Her eyes widen in delight. "Does he know you love her? Does she know?"

"Shush," I hiss, and she grins wide. "I don't fucking love Luna, okay. We just . . . well, we have history."

"Oh god, tell me the kid isn't yours?"

"Of course not. Do you think I'd still be alive if she was?"

She leans back in her chair and continues to smile. "I can't imagine you with a child."

"I'd be a shit dad."

"You think?" She suddenly looks more serious.

"There was no one to show me how to love as a kid," I admit, "so I don't reckon I could love my own."

"It can't be taught, Fletch. It comes naturally."

I stare out the window. "Yeah, well, what if it doesn't happen for me and I have a kid who I can't love?"

"Is that why you've never settled down?" she asks, her tone gentler.

"Do you think you'd have had kids with your kinky ex?"

She laughs. "No, probably not. We're both too career focussed."

"He's a surgeon, right?"

She nods. "He was going into private work, lip fillers and stuff. He wanted to open his own surgery."

"And he had no interest in kids?"

"Maybe." She shrugs, her nose scrunching slightly.

"We didn't discuss it properly, but I have a feeling he would've wanted me tied to the house the second I married him. He always loved the idea of dinner parties and me waiting for him at the door each evening. Of course, I was always working too, and he hated that."

Luna comes over and places a tray of warm bread and dips between us. "Hi," she says, smiling at Gemma.

"Hi," she replies. "This smells amazing."

"Just give me a shout when you want topping up." Then, she heads back into the kitchen.

"I can see why she appeals to you," Gemma says, bringing me from watching Luna. "She's pretty."

"If Grizz hears you, he'll break my fingers," I tell her, grabbing a chunk of bread and dipping it in the vinegary oil. "And probably scoop out my eyeballs with a spoon."

"Tell me what happened between you, so my life doesn't seem so tragic."

I sigh, chewing the bread before saying, "We fucked is all."

"Bullshit. You caught feelings."

"Maybe," I admit, shrugging. "But she loves Grizz, and he loves her. I missed out cos I was always thinking with my dick and not my heart."

"Who do you fuck now?" she asks, biting into some of the bread.

"What?" I ask, almost choking.

"Don't you have club bunnies, or whatever you call them, to meet your every need?"

I laugh. "Yeah, we do. And currently, I ain't fucking anyone but you."

She almost smiles again. "Don't be reading into it," she

says, smirking. "I don't need you getting attached or anything."

I laugh louder and she joins me. "You planning on breaking my heart, Snap?"

She nods. "I owe you one."

"Yah know," I say, pausing to look her in the eyes, "it's easy to forget we're supposed to be enemies when we're like this."

Her smile fades. "Take out all the bullshit and we're just two old friends catching up."

"It's like old times, though, like we were never apart."

"Things seemed to get serious between us really quickly back then. One minute, we were having fun together, and the next . . ." She trails off. "Well, the next, you got cold feet and ran."

"I didn't run, and we don't need to go over it again. I already apologised for being a prick. You've forgiven me anyway, remember?"

She smirks. "I don't remember forgiving you."

"Tell me about your job."

She takes another chunk of bread and pulls it apart, placing smaller pieces into her mouth. "Now you wanna talk about my job?" She grins.

"What made you join up?"

"I wanted to prove myself."

"To your father?"

She nods. "I wanted him to see I wasn't a fuck-up, but it didn't matter in the end. He still thinks I am, and I've done more than enough to prove him wrong, but he doesn't want to see it."

"You were so secretive back when you were a teenager, and you always seemed terrified of him."

## Gemma

I STARE DOWN into my drink. I'd love to open up and tell Fletch all about my father and everything he's ever done to break my heart, but then I'd have to be honest about Ruby, and that's something I'll never tell him.

I knock my drink back, enjoying the buzz I feel as the warmth hits me. "Refill?" I ask, standing.

He shakes his head, and I go over to the bar. The alcohol is running through my veins, and I feel braver as I place my empty on the bar top. "Well, well, well, if it isn't little Miss Raider," Grizz drawls, grabbing the whiskey bottle.

"That's it?" I ask with a laugh. "That's all you could come up with?"

"I got plenty of names, sweetheart, but all of them seem too good for you."

"What is it you hate so much, Grizz? My job, or the fact your Enforcer is fucking me?"

"Why would I give a shit if he's fucking you?" he snaps, topping up my glass.

I smile. "Aw, that's right, cos if he's fucking me, it means he isn't lusting after your old lady, right?"

His eyes narrow. "What's that s'posed to mean?"

"Can I get that?" I glance to my left at the biker who's almost pressed to my side and arch a brow. "Nyx," he introduces, winking.

"I can pay for my own drink," I say cooly.

"I didn't ask if you could afford it," he tells me, placing a bank note on the bar and sliding it to Grizz, who snatches it and rings it through. I look back over my shoulder to find the table where I left Fletch empty. "He asked me to keep you company," Nyx tells me, "He had to take a call."

"I can look after myself," I mutter, taking my drink.

Nyx slides his arm around my waist. "Look, ignore the VP, he's a dick sometimes," he almost whispers, glancing to Grizz to make sure he doesn't overhear. "But Fletch is a good judge of character, and if he likes you, so I do." I relax slightly and half smile. Nyx pulls out the stool beside him. "Take a seat. Watch me drink myself into oblivion."

"Oh yeah?" I ask, sliding onto the stool. "What are you drinking to?"

He leans over the bar and grabs a bottle of sours and two shot glasses. "Fuck knows. Maybe you can come up with a reason."

I watch as he pours two shots and slides one to me. "Oh, I don't really want—"

"You can't let me drink alone. Besides, stolen shots are the best." I smirk and knock it back, wincing at the sweet taste. "That was to new friendships," Nyx announces, topping both glasses up again. He picks one up and nods at me to do the same. He gently knocks my glass with his and asks, "Now, what are we drinking to?"

I think before replying, "Dumping cheating exes."

"Hell yeah."

My mobile vibrates in my bag, and I pull it out to see Karen's name on the screen. "Shit," I murmur. "I have to take this."

I slip off the stool and head for the bathroom. "Hi, Karen," I answer, trying to sound unwell.

"How's the migraine?" she asks.

"Not great," I mutter. I hate lying, especially to my boss, but I just couldn't face work tonight.

"I spoke with your father," she announces, and I cringe. "He told me you were fine earlier. He also mentioned you were having problems at home."

"Jesus," I mutter, staring at my tired face in the mirror. "Why would he tell you that?"

"Maybe he's worried?"

I roll my eyes. He's never worried a day in his life, especially not for me. "Look, Peter and I have split up, but I'm fine. I just needed a day to get myself together."

"Oh, Gem, I'm so sorry. Is there anything I can do?"

"No, I'm fine. It was a long time coming."

"Take some time off," she says gently.

"No."

"Your father thought it would be best, and I agree with him."

"I don't need time off. I'm fine. I'll be back tomorrow."

She sighs. "Okay, but the offer is there, and if I think you need it, I'm going to make it happen."

I disconnect and groan. He's looking to get me off this case.

When I return to the bar, Fletch is back, and he and Nyx are now sitting at the table together. I sit beside Fletch, and he smiles, throwing an arm around the back of my chair. It's an alpha move, reminding me of when he was younger.

"Tell me about how you two met," Nyx says, topping up my shot glass.

"No," says Fletch firmly.

I laugh, nudging him playfully. "Don't be so grumpy. Fletch was the local bad boy."

Nyx grins. "Really? Tell me more."

"All the girls loved him," I say in a teasing tone, "and he was always in trouble with the police."

# CHAPTER 10
### Fletch

I listen as Gemma tells Nyx the version of events how she remembers them. I remember them differently.

"He was in the back of my father's police car when he stopped to speak to me."

He'd demanded she go home because, in his opinion, she was dressed like a slut. She wasn't. She'd been wearing leggings and a shortish jumper that rode up when she moved, showing a slight bit of her stomach. *"You're too fat to wear that,"* he'd hissed, and I remember her looking so mortified, it made me want to smash his face into the steering wheel.

"Anyway, then he popped up everywhere, and before I knew it, he'd worked his sweet charm, and I was kissing him behind an abandoned house."

It was my house, but the second she'd screwed her nose up as we walked up the drive, I panicked and told her it was some derelict house and we just hung out around the back. I never took her back there after that, and I avoided all talk about my family.

"How old were you?" asks Nyx, and I can see the lust

in his eyes. He's warming up, and I shouldn't be pissed about it—after all, I texted him and told him to come here so we could put the plan into action. But now, as he leans closer to her, his eyes fixed on hers like whatever she says is the most important thing in the world, jealousy is burning through my veins.

"I was sixteen, and Fletch was twenty."

Nyx's brows shoot up. "Damn, brother, she was barely legal." I don't smile as they both laugh. Instead, I knock my drink back. "Next, you'll tell me you were a virgin," he adds, and Gemma presses her lips into a fine line, her cheeks pinking slightly. "Fuckkkk, you lucky son of a bitch."

"Is this all necessary?" I snap, unable to hold it in. "This getting to know us part?"

Nyx smirks, settling back in his chair and eyeing me for a minute. "You wanna step out, bro? Talk about it?"

"Talk about what?" asks Gemma.

"No, I don't. Change the fucking subject," I mutter, grabbing the bottle of sours from him and taking a swig.

"Easy, tiger, you'll not be able to perform for the lady if you carry on," he teases, and I slam the bottle down. He grins. "You want me to speak to the Pres and explain the situation has changed?"

"Am I missing something?" asks Gemma.

I stare at her as she waits for me to answer. Then, without thinking, I take a handful of her hair and tip her head back slightly, kissing her hard. When I pull back, there's heat in her eyes and she's breathless. "What was that for?" she whispers.

"Being so fucking hot," I tell her, taking another drink.

Nyx stands. "I'll be at the bar."

"What's going on between you?" asks Gemma.

I sigh. "Long story."

"I got the impression you were friends, but that didn't seem friendly."

"Remember when I said I've had threesomes?" She nods, and then it dawns on her and her mouth falls open slightly.

"Oh, with Nyx?"

"Sometimes, yeah, and I think he thought he'd try his luck with you."

Her cheeks burn brighter as she glances back towards the bar, where Nyx is in a deep conversation with Grizz. I'm sure the fucker is telling him I'm about to pull the agreement, but like fuck I am. "Doesn't it get weird?" she asks, her voice quieter.

"Me and Nyx?" I shake my head. "Nah. He stays at his end, and I stay at mine." I laugh for extra measure, trying to relax her and show it's no big deal. "Now, finish your drink. We're done here."

---

We get back to Gemma's, and I linger in the doorway. "Is lover boy likely to return?" I ask.

"Are you scared?" she teases.

I smirk. "Nope, but if I hit him, are you gonna arrest me?"

She laughs as I follow her inside. "Yes."

"You got any cuffs laying around?" I ask casually, and she looks back over her shoulder at me. "Hey, don't judge. Having you cuff me before was hot. I've relieved myself more than once thinking about it."

"It wasn't supposed to be hot."

"Well, if you were going for scary, you failed," I tell her, rushing her until she's pressed against the back of the couch. My hand trails across her stomach and under her top, tugging her bra down and cupping her breast. "Now, tell me where you keep those cuffs."

"Bag," she whispers, kicking a large black bag at side of the couch. I reach into it, not bothering to release her. When I pull out everything but the cuffs, I tip it up, emptying the contents to the floor. There's a brown file amongst the debris, and I push it out of view and under the couch before taking the cuffs. "Now, Officer Stone, you have the right to remain silent," I tell her while slipping the first cuff around her wrist. "Anything you do say, may be given in evidence." I secure the other cuff and pull her arms up her back until she gasps. "The things I could do right now, while you're defenceless and at my mercy . . ." I lift her top and unclip the front fastening on her bra. I pinch her nipples, and she shudders, pushing her backside against my semi-erect cock. "Now, get on your fucking knees," I hiss in her ear.

She does it without question, turning and dropping down in front of me as I release my erection. "Open," I order. She does, and I force my cock into her mouth, tipping her head back and groaning in pleasure as the warmth of her throat closes up at the intrusion. And just when I'm close to coming, I haul her up and push her over the couch so her backside is up in the air. I bury myself inside her, lost in the sensation of her.

"Condom," she pants, using her legs to try and kick me away.

I smirk, pulling her back to her knees, "I ain't coming

inside you, Snap," I pant, pressing my wet cock to her lips. She takes me, sucking me clean and draining me dry.

I'm aware she hasn't come, but it's all part of the plan. I need her to be eating out the palm of my hand, and for that, she needs to hear me. I lead her to the couch, and she lies down. I pull her to the very edge and drop to my knees, spreading her legs.

"Seeing you with Nyx tonight . . ." I begin, rubbing my thumb over her swollen clit. She hisses, closing her eyes. "Made me wonder what it would be like to watch him fuck you." I push a finger inside and find she's wet. "While you're sucking on my cock." I insert a second finger, and she moans. "Would you like that, Snap? Two men worshipping you?" She moans again. "I need words, Gem," I whisper, moving my mouth close enough for her to feel the warmth of my breath against her pussy.

A breathy 'yes' falls from her lips, and I lick her opening, tasting her juices on my tongue. "Do you think you can take us both together?" I ask, moving my fingers faster.

She's climbing, and small gasps of pleasure leave her lips one after the other. "Maybe I can take you here," I add, pressing my thumb to her tight backside. It's enough to send her over the edge, and she cries out, shuddering as wetness coats my fingers. "Damn, Snap, that's the hottest thing I've ever seen," I say, licking my fingers clean as I rise to my feet.

I go the bathroom to clean up and when I open the door, she's there, waiting to do the same. "Do you want to stay over?" she asks, not quite meeting my eyes. "I mean, you don't have to or anything. It's totally up to you."

"I wasn't planning on leaving yet, Snap. I haven't finished with you."

---

I CAN FEEL the questions on her mind because she isn't relaxing against my chest like before. "Spit it out," I tell her, stroking my hand lazily up and down her back. Having her pressed against me naked makes me want to repeat what we just did all over again, but we're both exhausted.

"Were you serious?" she asks.

"About?"

"You know what about," she huffs.

I smirk. "Nyx?"

"Yes."

"Absolutely not," I tell her.

"Oh."

"You wanna tell me why you sound so disappointed by that?" She's playing right into my hands and she doesn't even see it.

"I mean, you've done it before, so why not with me?"

I arch a brow and stare at her until she looks away, embarrassed. "You remember why you moved back here, right? Your job?"

"You keep telling me I'm wasting my time, so if there's nothing criminal going on, I'm not doing anything wrong."

I shrug. "Fine. If that's what you want."

Her head whips around to look at me again. "Is it what you want?"

My heart twists painfully in my chest. "I'm up for it," I lie.

She bites on her lower lip, smiling coyly. "Okay, then . . . great."

## Gemma

I TAP my fingers on the desk, waiting for my Chief Super. When she enters the meeting room, I drag my hand into my lap to stop the nervous fidgeting that'll no doubt give my game away. "Are you feeling better?" she asks, taking a seat opposite me.

I give a nod. "Yeah. Did I miss much?"

She shakes her head. "Have you got any news on Operation Sapphire? I'm meeting with the powers that be later today, and it would be nice if I could give them something."

"I haven't really had a chance to interact, what with Pete and everything," I lie.

"Maybe we're due another raid?"

I give a stiff nod. "Usually, weekends are busier, I believe."

"What about their businesses? Would it be worth watching those for a while?"

I shrug. "We tried that in the beginning. Phil had surveillance on their massage place."

"The whorehouse?"

I give a nod. "Although, on that day, they were massaging clients. They're always one step ahead. It's like they know all our moves."

She sighs heavily. "If we don't find something soon,

you know your father will pull the case. We've spent too long on it to come up with nothing, not even a wrap of weed."

"I'll speak to Phil, and we'll get a new plan together."

---

I FIND Phil at his desk scrolling through CCTV. I perch on the edge and ask, "What are you looking for?"

"Just the movements of the bikers, mainly the VP or the Enforcer."

"Oh?" I peer closer at the screen, trying to calm my racing heart. "Anything I should know about?"

"We had a team briefing yesterday, and Kay mentioned we had all this footage come in that hadn't been viewed. And seeing as my partner in crime was a no-show yesterday, I thought I'd make a start."

I scoff. "Don't we have someone from downstairs who can do this?"

He shakes his head. "Nope. Short staffed, apparently."

I get a glimpse of Fletch and my heart almost stops. "Where is this?" I ask.

"The Bar."

I stand abruptly. "How about I take over and you take a break?"

"I'm fine," he mutters, making a note on his pad.

"I insist," I say more forcefully, and he glances up, frowning. I force a smile. "To make up for my no-show yesterday."

He grins. "Fine, whatever." He unplugs the USB stick and hands it to me followed by his notes. "I've got to put some hours into some of my other cases anyway."

I head over to my own desk. "Who even asked for all the CCTV to be collected?" I ask casually.

He laughs. "Are you pissed you didn't think of it?"

"Not at all, but it's my investigation and I didn't ask for it."

"Karen got a uniform on it yesterday. Apparently, the order came from higher up."

I briefly close my eyes. "Right."

---

I SPEND a few hours staring at the black and white images of people coming and going from The Bar. It's tedious, and I lose count of the amount of coffee I've gone through just to stay awake.

I'm watching the footage from Anna's hen night when I spot my father breezing through the office. I pause the screen and rush after him, taking him by surprise when I slam the conference room door closed so we're alone.

"Gemma?"

I begin to close the blinds so my colleagues can't see from their desks. "Why did you ask for the CCTV to be checked on my case?"

He lowers into a chair, giving me that irritated look he saves especially for me. "I should be asking why you didn't."

"Because I didn't think it was important yet. We don't have anything, and trawling through hours upon hours of footage when we have no idea what we're looking for is a painstaking task."

"The footage may throw something up."

"And it might not," I snap. "I've wasted four hours

already watching drunks come and go from The Bar. We haven't even touched the garage or the other businesses."

"Gemma, you're a police officer, half your job is surveillance."

I narrow my eyes. "I'm a Detective Inspector. Uniforms trawl footage."

"So, get them on it."

"They don't have the staff and you know it. You're looking for something . . . you don't trust me."

"Gemma, if that was true, I'd have my own guys looking through it. But you're running out of time. If you don't get something soon, I'll have no choice but to close this case."

"Why? You know they're behind most of the drugs on the streets. If we keep up the pressure, they'll spill over. You're trying to sabotage this for me."

"Why would I do that?" he asks, sounding more irritated by the second.

"Because you can't stand to see me pull this off. You've wanted that club for ages. Plus, you promised them there wouldn't be another fuck-up when you stepped into this role."

He scoffs. "And then they hired you."

"I can get them," I yell.

"No, Gemma. No, you can't," he says calmly as he pushes to his feet. He rests his hands on the desk and glares at me. "You will fuck this up, and I'll be the one looking like a fool . . . again. You're right, I made a vow that I'd get rid of that biker club and clear our streets of drugs and guns. So far, you've come up with nothing. Nothing!" He slams his hand on the table. "And my job is at risk as well as yours."

I shake my head. "I didn't make any promises, and when I took this job, it wasn't to get the Demons. I was offered the case and I took it. I won't lose my job if I don't produce them."

He smirks. "If I lose my job, I'll be taking you down with me. You're running the case, and I'll ensure your name is on everyone's lips when we talk about failure."

I storm from the room and head straight for the bathroom, ignoring everyone's eyes on me as I pass.

I slam the door and brace myself against the wash basin. *That fucking bastard.* I close my eyes and take deep breaths, just the way my therapist taught me to whenever I get into an altercation with my father. It happened often when I was younger.

*I'm in my happy place, my face tipped up towards the sky and my eyes closed as the sun warms my skin. Here, like this, I can almost forget the way Fletch is pulling away from me. I'm terrified he's going to leave me. He's already talked about moving to London.*

*"Gemma?" My eyes shoot open at the sound of my father's voice, and as he rounds the corner, I scramble to my feet and stand straight. "Gemma," he barks, setting his eyes on me.*

*"What are you doing here?" I ask, my voice quivering from fright.*

*"I went through this," he snaps, holding up my mobile phone. I gasp, feeling my back pockets to make sure it's definitely my phone. Shit. How did I forget that?*

*"The allotment at five," he reads. "Get some more condoms, we're out." My face burns as I stare down at my feet. "Tell me it's not that feral little bastard off the estate."*

"My phone is private," I whisper. "I'm eighteen."

"Just," he spits, "and while you're living under my roof, you'll live by my rules. I checked your bank statement. You rent this space." It's not a question, but I nod. "Why?"

"I wanted to grow flowers," I mutter feebly.

"Flowers," he hisses, looking round at the array of different-coloured tulips. "I thought you'd gotten over this crap."

"There's no harm in growing them."

"Pull them up," he orders.

I frown. "What?"

"After all, you won't have time to look after them once this is born," he yells, throwing a piece of white plastic at my feet. I'm frozen to the spot, staring down at the positive pregnancy test. "I went through your room," he adds, sneering. "Read every diary, every fantasy." I pray for the ground to swallow me whole. Just remembering some of the things I wrote makes my face burn with embarrassment. I didn't expect my private thoughts to be read by anyone, least of all my father. "So, pull them up."

"No," I whisper, allowing tears to fall down my face.

He marches to me, and I flinch as he grabs my upper arms and forces me to my knees. "Pull them up, or I will have that little fucker arrested for grooming my daughter."

"He didn't groom me," I spit, and he slaps me. It's so hard, I instantly vomit into the dry soil.

"Your mother had stupid dreams of flower shops, look how that ended up."

I wipe my tears as I retch again, wincing as my fingers trace the burning of his slap. My mother loved her shop, but it's where she met the man of her dreams, leaving me *and my father behind when she moved to Spain to set up a new shop and life there. Since then, she's not been in contact, and that's probably down to my father.*

*The sound of his belt unclipping has me reaching for the red tulips, and as I tug them from the ground, I sob uncontrollably. His slaps always sting, but his belt hurts so much worse. And while I rip each pretty flower from the soil, I promise myself that one day, I'll have my own garden where I can grow whatever I want.*

# CHAPTER 11
**Fletch**

I wipe my hands on a rag and throw it over my shoulder. "I can have it ready for you by tomorrow," I tell the guy who's pacing the garage floor in agitation. "I can't do it today cos I don't have the parts." He rolls his eyes and stomps off to make a call.

Nyx smirks. "Every fucker thinks we're magic and can just fix everything with a simple touch."

"Life would be easier if we could."

"You talk to Gemma yet?"

I stick my head back under the bonnet to hide my irritation. "Not yet," I lie. I've decided I need some time on my own with her before I ruin it all. "I will, though."

"We could hang out together," he suggests, and I straighten up to stare at him.

"What are we, five?"

He shrugs with a slight smirk on his lips. "Maybe she needs some persuading from the master." I grab the rag from my shoulder and throw it in his face. He catches it, laughing.

"I've got it under control. She's putty in my hands, trust me."

Nyx stares past me and groans. "What the fuck?"

I turn to find police cars pulling up on the forecourt. "Great," I mutter, watching as officers pile out and head our way. A second later, Gemma pushes her way through them, holding up her badge. "D.I. Stone," she says firmly, avoiding eye contact. "We've got a warrant to search these premises."

"Seriously?" I bark, and she briefly glances at me. For once, she looks unsure and maybe a little guilty.

"Is there anyone else on the premises?" asks another man, joining Gemma.

"Nope," I state.

"Someone cuff them," Gemma says, stepping away.

I'm cuffed and jostled into the office with Nyx, where we're both forced to take a seat. "What grounds have you got to search?" I ask the nearest officer.

"We believe you're involved in criminal activities," he says, pulling open a filing cabinet and searching through the paper files.

"You won't find shit," I snap.

"Relax," mutters Nyx. "They want to rile you."

"They're putting off potential customers," I snap. "This is a fucking joke."

"We'll get the bitch back," he murmurs, adding a wink.

Half an hour passes before Gemma enters the office while the rest of the officers congregate outside. "Here's the paperwork," she mutters, placing a folded piece of paper on the desk. She proceeds to unlock Nyx's cuffs and then moves to me. "I didn't have a choice," she almost whispers.

I stand abruptly, and she takes a step back. "Fuck you, Gem," I hiss, pushing past her and stepping out into the fresh air. "Ain't it time you fuckers got off my property?" I yell at the officers mulling around.

I feel her step out behind me. "Your attitude isn't helping," she mutters quietly so only I can hear.

"Just go," I snap, keeping my back to her.

"I'll call."

"Don't fucking bother. Whatever this was, it's done." I head back inside, slamming the door hard in her face.

"Shit, brother, she looks gutted," says Nyx, staring out the window.

"We need a new plan. I'm done."

"Bullshit. We can't just change the plan."

I glare at him. "Why are you so bothered? Are you that desperate to get in her pants?"

He smirks, and it makes me want to smash his face in. "Don't you wanna crush her, Fletch, after what she's just done?"

I scrub my hands over my face. "I have a kilo of powder in the roof tiles," I almost whisper.

His eyes widen. "What the fuck?" he growls, glancing nervously behind me. "Axel told you to clear all your shit up. He told everyone."

"I know," I hiss. "It was a last-minute thing, and I didn't expect her to come here."

"You fucking idiot. Get rid of it, now."

"I can't," I snap. "What if they're watching us? They'll know we're spooked and expect us to make a move."

"Axel will break your jaw for this bullshit," he yells, storming back into the office.

My phone rings out and I pull it from my pocket to see

Gemma's name flashing. I cancel the call. A second later, a text message comes through.

> Snap: You're damn lucky I didn't bring dogs with me today. Whatever you're hiding, get rid of it now.

I stare at the text until Nyx returns a few minutes later. "Axel is going off his head. He's calling church."

"She knows," I mutter, turning the phone to him so he can read the text message.

"Church," he barks, pulling the shutters down.

---

AXEL PACES the spot behind his chair. It's a sure sign he's pissed, and when he fixes his dark, angry eyes on me, I almost choke on the air that's threatening to suffocate me. "I'm sorry," I begin. It was the wrong thing to say, and he slams his fist into my jaw, almost knocking me off my chair. "Shit," I hiss, shaking my head and cupping my chin.

The rest of the brothers keep their eyes downcast as he goes back to pacing.

"Nyx said you got a text," says Grizz.

I give a slight nod and produce my phone. He reads it and shows Axel. "You're a stupid idiot, you know that," Duke tells me. "You think any of us are happy about putting shit on hold?"

"I forgot it was there," I mutter feebly.

"Damn, brother, are you that loaded that you can stash a kilo and forget about it?" sneers Grizz.

"I fucked up," I admit. "I'm sorry."

"This warning," says Axel, sliding my phone back to me, "you think she's watching the place so you move it and then she can swoop in?"

I shrug. "Maybe."

"When are you next seeing her?" asks Grizz.

"Never. I'm done with her," I tell him.

I don't see Axel's fist this time, and it's not until I'm on my back staring up at the ceiling that I realise he got me good. My eye throbs, and I slam my foot hard on the floor to keep my calm. "Stay there," he hisses, pointing a finger in my face. I clench my jaw to stop myself spouting some remark that'll just earn myself a full-on beating. "You don't call the shots here, I do. She wants to take this club down, so you don't get to decide if you're done with her. We continue with the plan."

"And the drugs?" I ask.

He holds out a hand, and I grab it warily. He pulls me to my feet, and I sit back in my chair. "You move them when she's with you."

"What?" I ask, my brows reaching my hairline.

"She knows you're hiding something. If she comes back tomorrow with a dog, you're done. You move the stuff while she's with you. Drop it at the gym and place it in this locker." He passes me a key with a number on it. "Tell her it's a clean set of gym clothes you keep there for whenever you want to drop in the gym. Shadow is gonna do what he does best," he says, slapping Shadow on the back. "He'll get some shots of you two together. She can't deny being involved if she's with you."

I bury my face in my hands then nod. "Okay." It's a good plan, and if this all comes crashing down, her case against us will fall apart. "I'll call her now."

"No," says Nyx. "She was gutted earlier when you rejected her. Let her come to you. It's less suspicious."

"Listen to him," says Grizz. "He knows what he's talking about."

Nyx grins, nudging his shoulder into mine. "I'm the master," he whispers. "Told yah."

### Gemma

I WALK around the car for a third time. I have no idea what I'm doing, but I'm hoping this makes it look like I do. I groan because who the hell am I kidding? I've never purchased a brand-new car before. My last was second-hand, and I kept that until it died. I pull out my mobile and send off a picture to Fletch, hoping he'll offer some words of advice.

The sleezy salesman makes his way back to me with a huge shit-eating grin on his face. "Wanna go for a ride?" He dangles a key in the air.

"Actually, I'm waiting for my friend to message me back. He knows more about cars than me." I glance at my phone and will it to light up. I know Fletch is mad at me, and I get it, but he knew my job before he slept with me and I never promised to back off. With my father and Karen breathing down my neck, it was unavoidable.

"It's hard to make a decision without feeling the power of the engine rumbling through your body." He scans me with his beady eyes for extra measure.

The sound of a motorbike fills the air, and I pray it's him coming to my rescue. A minute later, Nyx stalks in as he pulls off his helmet. "Let's go," he says clearly.

"Go where?" I ask.

"This piece of shit will rip you off," he says, grabbing my hand.

"Hey, that's slander," the car salesman yells after us.

Nyx gets on his bike and passes me the spare helmet. "Where did you come from?" I ask, wondering how he got here so fast.

"I was in the area, so Fletch sent me to get you."

"Oh." I throw my leg over the bike and push the helmet on. Nyx pulls me closer to him, just like Fletch does, and then he pulls my arms around his waist and starts the bike.

A few minutes later, we're pulling into the clubhouse. I glance around nervously as I step off the bike. I've been lucky so far, not getting caught with Fletch, but it's the middle of the day, and who knows what my father could have put in place behind my back.

Fletch is talking to a woman when we go inside. He's laughing with her and jealousy instantly burns me. He glances my way before turning his attention back to her. I wait a few minutes before he finally heads my way. "Everyone knows that jackass on the High Street is a rip-off."

"Clearly not everyone," I mutter.

"I've gotta stop by the garage to get my gym bag, then I'll take you to a decent salesman."

"Thank you."

He makes no move to grab my hand as he leads me back out to his bike. He climbs on without helping me with the helmet, and when I slide on behind him, he doesn't grab my legs the way he usually would to drag me closer. In fact, when I take hold of the bar behind me, I fully expect him to pull my arms around his waist, but he doesn't and I'm disappointed. Somehow, I've fallen back into Cameron Fletcher's trap.

We stop at the garage, and he runs inside, returning seconds later with a gym bag. He lays it across my lap and gets back on the bike. "Shouldn't we secure this?" I ask.

"You'll have to hold on to it."

"I can't, I'll fall off the bike."

He sighs heavily, like I'm suddenly a huge pain in his side, before taking my arms and pulling me a little closer so the bag is trapped between our bodies. "Better?" he spits, and my heart aches.

Next, we stop at a car sales garage. A man steps out the office dressed casually. He doesn't look like a salesman, which instantly relaxes me. He shakes hands with Fletch, looking genuinely pleased to see him. "This is Gemma," says Fletch without looking my way. "She needs a reliable car, and I know you'll look after her."

"Of course, brother."

Fletch waits by the office, staring down at his mobile phone, and the salesman smiles. "I'm Darren."

"Hi," I mutter, unable to hide the hurt in my voice. Suddenly, I'm less excited about buying a car. I don't like the way I feel when Fletch is being so cold and distant because it shouldn't bother me nearly as much as it does.

Darren proceeds to show me around his showroom of shiny cars. He doesn't push me on any but talks about the pros and cons of the ones I like. I finally settle on an Audi, and when I glance back to ask Fletch's opinion, I see he's talking on his phone. "I'll just take it," I mutter, offering a weak smile.

"I'll sort the paperwork."

When I finally step back out the office, Fletch is waiting for me on his bike. The car needs to be registered, so I've got to collect it tomorrow. "Done?" he asks.

"Yeah, thanks."

"Let me drop this at the gym and I'll take you home."

"I can walk," I say, not wanting to be in his cold presence for a second longer.

"Get on the fucking bike, Gemma." It's the first time he's been so stern with me that, for a second, I hesitate. "Now."

We stop by the gym, and again, he rushes inside to dump his bag. Then he drives to my place and gets off the bike after me. He follows me up the path, and while I unlock the door, I think of excuses to deter him from coming inside, but when I turn to tell him, he grabs me by the throat and pushes me backwards into the house. It's not aggressive but commanding, and I'm instantly weak at the knees as his mouth clashes with mine in a hungry, claiming kiss.

He rips my shirt open, tugging it from my arms and discarding it on the floor. He kicks my legs apart and his hand rubs between my legs. Even through my leggings, it's effective, and I cling to his shoulders as he rubs faster. He slams me against the wall and crouches in front of me, gripping the material between my legs and pulling it hard enough to rip a hole there. I gasp as he moves my underwear to one side and presses his mouth to my pussy, hungrily licking me.

"Jesus, Fletch," I cry, pressing my hands to his head to hold him closer. It all feels so rushed and desperate, yet I can't stop the excitement it's evoking from me. I come hard, crying out while he eats my pussy with a starved hunger.

Before I'm fully recovered, he stands, and I watch through hooded eyes as he sheathes his erection with a condom and pushes it to my wet entrance. He slams into me with a grunt, leaning down to take my bra-covered breast into his mouth. He soaks the material with his tongue, gently biting on my erect nipple.

He lifts me and carries me through to the lounge. The curtains are open, and for a second, I worry someone passing will see us, but he forces me towards the window regardless and withdraws from me. He turns me to look outside, placing my hands on the windowsill. "Fletch," I murmur, about to protest, but he stuffs his erection back into me without warning and begins a punishing onslaught which consumes my entire being, making sure any protests die on my lips.

"You like the fucking power," he hisses, grabbing a handful of my hair and tipping my head back. "You like watching me squirm?"

My words won't come. He's fucking me too hard and too fast. All I can think about is the orgasm about to rip through me again. I feel his hands in the wetness between my legs, and then his finger is pressing at my tight backside. I fidget, getting distracted from my end goal but determined to stop him exploring there. He bats my hand away, continuing to press his finger to the tight hole. "Fletch," I whisper, resting my head on my arm.

"I'm in control," he hisses, and I cry out as the digit slips into me, causing an uncomfortable pain.

The front door opens and closes, and I freeze, my

impending orgasm ebbing away. "Surprise," whispers Fletch, still chasing his own release as he slams into me.

Nyx leans in the doorway, a smirk playing on his lips. "Looks like I'm just in time."

I feel the blush spread from my neck to my cheeks, but as Fletch continues to fuck me, I can't find the words to stop any of this.

# CHAPTER 12

**Fletch**

I don't stop fucking Gemma. Nyx shrugs from his kutte, his eyes fixed on us. I move us away from the window and drag her onto the couch, pulling her to sit over me. I grip her hips and move her, forcing her to ride me. She looks unsure, but I need to distract her while Nyx sorts out the recording device, so I pull her in for a kiss. He slips it between two books on the shelf and drops down on the chair opposite us.

I was so fucking angry, I'd called Nyx and arranged for him to turn up here. But fucking her like this feels wrong, and as she rides my cock with that uncertain mistrusting glint, I realise I can't look her in the eyes, so I grab her by the hair again and tip her head back. I catch Nyx's glare and give him the nod. He stands and slowly heads our way while popping the button on his jeans. I bite gently on her exposed nipple, and she shudders. Nyx runs his hands over her shoulders, sliding them around to her breasts. I release her hair, and she stares at me with eyes now full of lust as he teases her nipples between his thumb and finger.

I stare at his fingers working her into a frenzy and fight

the urge to stop this whole thing. His hand travels down her front, stopping on her clit. She cries out, closing her eyes but moving faster to chase her release. When his fingers are wet enough, he takes them to her backside, and she tenses. "Darlin', you gotta relax," he whispers in her ear.

I feel my cock soften. Knowing he's touching her is too much, and I grip her hips, stilling her. Her eyes shoot open, and she stares at me with worry. I don't bother to speak. I lift her from me and rest my head back on the couch, staring up at the ceiling and ignoring Nyx as he drops to his knees, no doubt wanting to taste her . . . to taste what's mine.

I ball my fists and count in my head to calm myself. I have to do this. The club is depending on me. "Stop," I hear her say, and it takes a second to register. "I just need . . . it's all going so fast."

I glance up to where Nyx is about to bury his face between her legs. "You heard," I snap. "Stop."

Nyx falls back, holding his hands up in surrender. "I heard her, man, relax."

He pushes to his feet and moves back to the chair. Gemma stands, gives me a sad smile, and leaves the room.

"It's too much too soon," I mutter.

"You sure about that?" asks Nyx, cocking a brow. "I saw how tight your fists were just then, brother. You wanted to smash them into my face. You like her."

I pinch the bridge of my nose. "You're talking shit. Leave us."

He grabs his kutte and fastens his jeans. "You know where I am when you're ready." He laughs. "I mean, when she's ready." He takes the camera. "We might have enough, and Shadow got some shots of you two in the window and her holding the bag on the back of your bike."

"Wait," I mutter, standing. I feel beneath the couch and find the paper file I kicked under there. "It's got my name on it," I say, passing it to him. "Take it to the club."

I find her in the kitchen drinking a glass of water. "He's gone."

She starts at my words and places the glass on the side. "He didn't have to leave. I just needed a minute."

"You wanna fuck him?" I bark and instantly regret it. It's not her fault I'm jealous.

She slowly shakes her head. "No."

"You fucked up coming to the garage," I yell, beginning to pace. "You sprung that shit on me, Gemma."

"It's my job," she snaps. "I was doing my job."

"I've gotta stop you," I say, running my hands through my hair. "The club is relying on me."

"Stop me how?"

"I don't know," I yell, "but please don't make me find out."

"There's nothing to hide," she snaps. "You said there was nothing."

"You know that's bullshit," I shout angrily.

"Stop talking," she hisses. "Don't tell me anything you can't take back."

"I wasn't meant to like you," I admit, leaning against the wall. I feel tired, and when my eyes meet hers, she looks exactly the same. "It will never work."

"Leave the club," she says.

I laugh. "If you knew me at all, you'd know that can never happen."

She rushes to me, grabbing a fistful of my shirt. "It can. Just leave and we can be together."

"It's my life," I snap, pushing her from me. "It's the only place I've ever felt like I belonged."

"And what about us? Don't I make you feel like that?"

"We can't even be out in public together. We couldn't fourteen years ago, and we still can't. Gemma, I can't give up the club. And if you felt anything at all for me, you'd never ask me to."

She sighs, her shoulders dropping slightly. "I need to get cleaned up," she mutters, passing me to head upstairs.

I follow a few minutes later and kick off my boots. I shrug from my kutte and lie on her bed. When she returns wrapped in a towel, I hold out my hand, which she takes. "I've never wanted to kill a brother before, but seeing Nyx touch you . . ." I trail off, and she climbs over me, allowing the towel to fall away.

"It felt wrong," she admits. "All I could think about was you and how I just need you."

My hand snakes around her neck and I pull her closer until our lips touch. "Just me," I whisper, kissing her gently.

I lay her on her back and slip from my shirt, followed by my jeans and boxers. I grab a condom from my back pocket and slip it over my erection before slowly crawling over her body. This time, when I sink into her, I whisper soft words into her ear about her belonging to me. And I make promises for the future. Promises I know I can't keep.

I WAITED until Gemma had fallen to sleep in my arms before carefully slipping out of there. I couldn't even face writing a note, because what the fuck would I say? Sorry?

I fix Axel with a glare. "Beat me to death if it makes you feel better, just know I'm out."

"So, you do like her?" asks Grizz, smirking.

"You got what you needed, right? She's implicated in the drugs, she's on tape fucking me, and you have photos. That's enough to use against her."

Axel gives a slight nod. "Grizz, give us a minute," he mutters, and Grizz leaves.

"Sit," he tells me, and I do. "Is he right, do you love her?"

I scoff, ready to deny it, but my smirk fades and I groan. "Yeah, Pres, I think I do."

"And she feels the same?"

I nod, my aching heart splitting some more. "When she wakes up to see I'm gone, she'll realise what just happened between us."

"What happened?"

"We said goodbye."

He gives a knowing nod and pushes to stand. "You need whiskey and pussy . . . in that order."

---

I CANCEL Gemma's call for the eighth time and go back to fixing the engine. When my life goes to shit, this is where I come to find peace. I know cars. I understand what makes them tick and how to fix them. Women, I haven't a clue.

A text comes through and I pull the screen down enough to read it without opening it.

> Snap: Raid. Tonight. Club.

*Fuck.* Now, she's giving me the heads-up. I call Axel to relay the information, but it makes no difference—the club is clean.

> Snap: Please answer. Talk to me.

There's only one way I can get her to walk away.

## Gemma

I don't know why I gave him the heads-up. I just wanted a response, seeing as he's clearly ignoring me. We made love. For the first time ever, we made love, and then I woke full of happiness, only to find him gone. He didn't even leave me a fucking note. I guess he didn't need to—it was clear what had happened.

He didn't respond to my tip-off anyway. Maybe he hasn't even seen it.

He's done. Just like before. And I'm in pain, just like before.

My mobile rings out and I step outside to answer. "I'm at work," I say cooly.

"I know," snaps my father, "but this is urgent. Ruby knows."

My world stands still. "What?"

"She found the paperwork, Gemma. I had no choice but to tell her everything."

"No," I hiss. "You promised she'd never find out."

"Just get here now." He disconnects.

I arrive at my father's house within ten minutes. He's waiting outside, pacing the porch. I stomp up the steps, and he finally stops in front of me. "Sarah left me," he says, and I still. "A few weeks ago," he adds. "I finally told Ruby, and she didn't take it well."

I frown. "Why did she leave?"

"Does it matter?"

"Yes."

"He was having an affair," snaps Ruby from the doorway, and we both turn to face her. "I know everything. Sarah told me."

I swallow the huge lump that's forming in my throat. "Let's go inside and talk."

"So you can tell me more lies?"

"We were protecting you," I begin, and she spins on her heel and heads back in. We follow, and for the first time, I feel like Father and I are a team.

She sits on the couch as Father goes to the window, keeping his back to us. I lower into the leather armchair. "I was too young," I begin.

"Bullshit," she hisses.

"Language," I remind her.

"Really?" she screams, taking me by surprise. "You hide this from me and you want me to watch my language? How about this . . . slag . . . fucking liar . . . dirty lying bitch."

"Stop," Father bellows, and I will her to before he slaps her. I remember how bad those hurt. He moves towards her, and I stand, ready to stop him. He eyes me before smirking. "She needs to know the sacrifices we made for her."

"I never asked you to," she yells.

He shoves me out the way, and I fall back into the chair. I watch as he grabs her arm and hauls her closer so they're practically nose-to-nose. "I gave you a decent life with parents who could raise you. She wasn't fit to," he spits, pointing in my direction but not moving his eyes from hers. "Sarah was a good mother."

"When she wasn't sleeping off her pills," Ruby yells.

"Maybe we should talk," I cut in, "just me and Ruby."

"Sister to sister," she hisses sarcastically.

My father pushes her to sit again and storms from the room. "You shouldn't antagonise him," I whisper.

"I'm not scared of him."

"Ruby, I didn't lie to hurt you. My life back then wasn't great."

"Why," she demands, "because he told you it wasn't?"

I shrug, biting my lower lip to stop the tears. "I was too young and too naïve. Your father," I take a breath, "well, he wasn't a good person, and I was heartbroken and not thinking straight. Our father . . . I mean, my father, offered to raise you with Sarah. It was the only way I could keep you in my life."

"You've lied to me my whole life," she whispers, her eyes full of pain.

I give a nod. "I'm not proud, but how could I tell you? Once it was decided, it was out of my hands." I allow the tears to slip down my cheeks. "I just knew I needed to keep you in my life, and this was the only way."

"I want to meet him," she announces. "My real father."

I begin to shake my head. "It's not a good idea. I don't even know where he is," I lie.

Her eyes narrow and guilt eats away at me some more. "No more lies," she whispers. "Please."

My heart twists painfully in my chest. "He's doesn't know about you," I admit.

A small sob escapes, and she sits up straighter. "Then you'd better tell him."

"I can't do that, Ruby. I can't have him around you when I know he's no good for you."

"And he was?" she hisses, pointing to the door my father exited through. "You thought I'd be better raised here with a mother who spends her life out of it on meds and him, a man who cheats constantly and talks to us like he actually hates us?"

"I didn't have a choice," I mutter feebly.

"Crap, absolute crap. I'm not staying here."

"You have to," I argue.

"I'm coming to yours."

"Ruby, he'll never allow it."

"He's not my real father," she suddenly screams. "And I can't look at him for a second longer. It's bad enough I have to look at you, but him . . . I fucking hate him. And if you make me stay here, I'll run away."

I sigh heavily and push to my feet. "I'll talk to him."

I find Father in the kitchen nursing a scotch. "Why didn't you tell me Sarah left?"

"I'm telling you now."

"And she didn't try to take Ruby?"

He shakes his head. "If we're honest, she never really took to her, did she? Jolene practically raised her, just like she did you."

"Ruby is insisting on coming back to mine for a while," I say cautiously.

"Fine. Whatever."

"Really?" I'm surprised, and I can't hide it from my voice.

"She's your daughter," he mutters.

I leave the room before he can change his mind and tell Ruby to pack some things.

---

I head back to work after I get Ruby settled. She isn't speaking to me, and I don't blame her. But as much as I want to spend the night trying to make her see things from my point of view, I think right now she just needs time. Besides, I have a raid to lead.

---

The Chaos Demons clubhouse is all quiet when we arrive at midnight. Maybe Fletch took note of my text after all.

We go through the side door again, just because it's the easiest route in. This time, I opted to take Fletch's floor. Simply because I need to see him. I purposely sent Phil on another floor because if he sees me talking to Fletch, he'll see the connection I've made.

I take a breath, glancing to my left, where my three officers are waiting on me to open the bedroom door. I push and reach for the light, bathing the room in a bright white glow. It takes me a second to work out the dynamics before me, and when I do, I almost want to vomit. Everything seems to move in slow motion.

Fletch is naked, and beside him is Nyx fucking a blonde. Fletch glances my way, not looking at all surprised. He throws the sheet back and swings his legs over the edge of the bed, holding out his wrists, ready to be cuffed.

Nyx groans, shuddering before grinning my way. "Sorry, needed to finish," he explains, before pulling from the girl and handing her a shirt.

"Stay where you are," I snap as Nyx moves to grab some shorts.

"Officer, I'm naked," he drawls. "Can I at least cover my junk, or are you enjoying the view too much?"

"Hurry the fuck up," I snap, pulling a set of cuffs from my belt and slapping them extra hard onto Fletch's wrists. "Someone cuff the others," I bark, pulling the cuffs so Fletch has to stand. "Line them up outside the room," I add.

I wait for them all to move out, and when Fletch goes to follow, I hold him back. He avoids my eyes. "Really?" I hiss. "You're just gonna act like you don't give a shit?"

He rolls his eyes, irritating me further. "Can we not do this now, Gemma?" The full use of my name hurts me more. "I mean, the constant texts were bad enough, but now, you're creating a raid to see me?"

I feel my cheeks redden. "Fuck you," I whisper, pushing him towards the door.

I stand in the doorway, watching the officers tip the room upside down. Of course, there's nothing apart from a blade under the mattress. I hold out an evidence bag for it to be placed inside, then I show it to Nyx and Fletch. "Who does this belong to?"

"Really?" mutters Fletch, arching a brow. "You're gonna arrest me for having a blade under my bed?"

I give a smile. "Yep." I turn to another officer. "Take him out to the van."

# CHAPTER 13
**Fletch**

I tap my fingers impatiently on the thin, rubber mattress. I hate the cells, and I've been sitting in this fucker for the last eight hours. When the lock in the door finally clanks, I stand, ready to give them a piece of my mind. I decide against it when Gem leans against the door frame.

"You ready for that interview?"

"Are you shitting me?" I snap. "It wasn't even out in public. What are you doing me for?"

"It's illegal to own a zombie knife in the UK."

"Okay, it's not mine."

"Nice try. Let's go," she says, smirking and putting the cuffs back on me.

I follow her into an interview room. "Yah know, it's illegal to fuck the man you have under surveillance."

"I haven't put you under surveillance," she retorts as we sit down. "You waivered your right to having a solicitor present, is that correct?"

"Cos I haven't done anything."

She presses the record button on the tape and opens her

note pad. "This evening, a knife was found under your mattress," she begins. "Does that knife belong to you?"

"No comment."

"Have you seen the knife before?"

"No comment."

"Has that knife been involved in any illegal activity?"

I roll my eyes. "No comment."

She sighs, leaning forward and resting her arms on the desk. "Listen, it's in your best interests to tell me if that knife has been involved in anything. We're going to run tests on it."

"No fucking comment," I say more clearly this time.

"It was found in your room. Did you know it's illegal to own a zombie knife?"

"No comment."

"Fine. Interview terminated at," she checks her watch, "seven-thirty-five." She turns the recording device off. "I'll take you back to your cell."

"This is stupid," I mutter, pushing to stand. "You're hurt, I get it, but all this is bullshit."

She grabs my cuffs roughly and shoves me towards the door. "Now, why would I be hurt?"

"You know why. But it was for the best. It was never gonna work long-term between us."

"Stop talking," she snaps, pulling the door open.

"You wouldn't want your colleagues to find out the truth, right?" I ask, sniggering.

She pushes me into my cell but remains in the doorway. "You're right, it was never going to work. I'll go back to my life, and you go back to yours."

I eye her suspiciously. "What do you mean?"

"Just what I said. I have stuff going on." She looks

away and her expression is troubled. Suddenly, I have the urge to know everything, but before I can ask, she forces a smile. "And I'd rather not make my life more complicated by chasing your club down. So, you win. Go back to your life and I'll leave you alone."

"Really?"

"The big man at the top won't fund this forever, and we've found nothing so . . ." she trails off. "Goodbye, Fletch."

She leaves, slamming the door and locking it. I sigh. If she's being honest, it's exactly what we wanted . . . so why the fuck does it feel so shit?

---

I'm released pending further enquires at eight a.m. that morning. They'll find nothing on the knife. It's brand new and purely for protection, and it's been under my mattress for months. I'd just forgotten about it and the last search wasn't thorough enough.

Axel is waiting outside the station in one of the club's cars. He gets out when he spots me. "You good?" I nod, getting in the car, and he does the same. "What the fuck was all that about?"

"I've been ghosting her," I admit. "She wasn't happy."

"Jesus, Fletch, why didn't you let her down gently?"

"Cos I thought it was better to just cut it off. Anyway, it doesn't matter. She's dropping her vendetta."

I feel his eyes on me. "Really?"

"I was suspicious too, but she told me the guys at the top won't fund it anymore. They haven't found anything, so she's stepping back."

"Do you believe her?"

"Yeah."

He smiles. "That'll do for me."

At the clubhouse, Nyx is still in my bed with whoever this latest conquest is. I give him a nudge, and he stirs, opening one eye and smiling. "You're back?"

"Why are you in here?" I ask, kicking off my boots.

"Didn't wanna ruin my sheets, Duchess said she's sick of washing them." He yawns, stretching out. "Did she get the message?"

I give a nod. "Yep. Think she got it loud and clear."

He grins. "I thought you'd cave and tell her you didn't fuck her."

I run my eyes over the sleeping blonde. "Nah, she needed to think the worst of me so she'd move on."

"Well, if that didn't do it, the recording certainly will."

I frown. "What are you talking about?"

"The sex tape. The police took it."

I freeze. "What?"

"They took it."

"How the hell did they find it?"

"They forced Axel to open the safe. It was in there."

I run my hands through my hair. "That was for us to use to get her to lay off, not for the police to find."

"Not much we can do about it now."

I groan. "Fuck. This will ruin her."

"Why do you care, brother? She's a copper. Fuck her."

I pull out my phone, but before I can text, Nyx snatches it. "Man, if you warn her, Axel will do his nut. You and her are done. Leave it at that and forget about her."

I get a few hours' sleep before Grizz is banging on doors calling church. By the time I head downstairs, everyone is seated.

Axel slams the gavel down to start the meeting. "As you can see, Fletch survived a night in the cells." He pats me on the back. "Released pending further enquires, but the knife is clean."

"The thing is, Pres, I got people pulling out of business cos they're sick of waiting," says Atlas. "How long is this gonna go on?"

"That's what we're here for," he says with a grin. "We reckon it's done. The copper told Fletch the funding was pulled from the investigation. So, although we still gotta lay low, we can start moving gear again." The men cheer, but for some reason, I don't share their happiness. "And when they view that footage, anything she's got on us will be pulled."

"Did you hand it over?" I snap.

He smirks. "I may have pointed them in the direction."

I stand, slamming my hands on the table. "That was for us to use, and now she's backed off, we don't even need it."

He frowns, then also stands, matching my height. "You need to watch your tone, brother," he warns.

"You're gonna destroy her career," I yell.

He arches a brow. "She wanted to destroy my club."

"But she didn't," I argue.

"All's fair in love and war, right?"

"We need to get it back," I snap.

"We need to let fate decide."

"Pres, I'm serious, I can't let her go down like that."

"Your loyalty should be with this club," he snaps.

"It is. I just . . ." I sigh, flopping down in my seat. "She's suffered enough."

"She's a copper, Fletch. Don't feel sorry for her sort," reasons Duke.

"And this will put an end to her having any thoughts about coming back for more."

## Gemma

I STARE BLANKLY at the ceiling. I got home hours ago, but I can't sleep. I saw Ruby off to school even though she never spoke a word to me, and now, my mind is thinking over every single bad decision I've ever made. I groan, rolling onto my side and picking up my mobile phone.

I type out a text and my finger hovers over the send button, but then I delete it. I can't tell him. I want to, and Ruby needs me to, but I just can't.

What if he wants to get to know her? What if he wants her to stay with him? I shudder. Thinking of Ruby in the clubhouse makes me feel sick. Sitting up, I start the text again. I have to try . . . for Ruby.

> Me: Can we meet to talk?

I fall into a disturbed sleep but only manage a few hours before I'm awake again and that sick feeling returns.

I check my phone and find no reply from Fletch. I'm disappointed, I can't lie.

Finding Ruby downstairs, I ask, "Did you have a good day at school?"

She glances up in that sulky way teenagers do but doesn't reply. I'm tired of being ignored by everyone in my life. "I've made contact with him," I blurt. "Your father." This gets her attention. "He hasn't texted me back yet."

"Did you tell him it was important? That it was urgent?"

I hate how desperate she sounds. "If he doesn't reply, I'll go and see him."

"If you know where he is, take me to him."

I shake my head. "I can't just turn up and spring you on him. He's . . . difficult."

"I don't care. I want to see him."

"Ruby," I say on a sigh, "please just let me do this my way."

"Go now," she snaps. "Go to him now and tell him so I know either way if he's interested in getting to know me."

"Is that what you want?" I ask.

"Yes."

"You won't even speak to me, but you want to know this stranger?"

"You lied. He didn't."

"So, now, I'm the enemy?"

"Just go and tell him," she repeats, turning away. "Please."

And that one word is all it takes to have me heading for the door. I've at least got to tell him, even if he doesn't want to know Ruby.

Smoke is on the gate, and when I pull up outside, he steps from the gatehouse. "What do you want?"

"To see Fletch."

"Too bad."

"Please," I say more urgently, "it's important."

He rolls his eyes and pulls out his mobile phone, tapping away. A few minutes later, I get a text message.

> Fletch: We made an agreement, Gemma.
> Go home.
>
> Me: I have to tell you something.
>
> Fletch: I don't want to hear it. We're over.
>
> Me: It's about our past. Why I went away.

A minute later, he stomps from the clubhouse and heads for the gates. He looks irritated, and I hate that he's treating me like a needy ex trying to ruin his day. "Gemma, this has to stop. You can't come here unannounced."

"Not without official papers at least," says Smoke, grinning.

We both stare at him in annoyance, and he shrugs, stepping back into the gatehouse.

"I don't want to be here," I snap. "I'm not trying to win you back, if that's what you think."

"Then why are you here?"

"Can we at least go somewhere to talk?"

He shakes his head. "No. You're not welcome in here."

"I can't say what I need to at the gate, Fletch."

"Then don't fucking tell me," he snaps, turning and heading back to the clubhouse.

"I got pregnant before," I blurt. He stops, keeping his back to me for at least a minute before slowly turning to face me. I swallow the huge lump forming in my throat.

"Open the gate," he barks in Smoke's direction.

The gate begins to creek as it opens, and the second he can step out, he grabs my arm and shoves me back towards my car. "Get in," he growls. He rounds the passenger side and gets in. "Drive."

"Where?"

"Your place."

"No. We can't go there."

He turns in his seat. "When? How?"

I grip the wheel, fixing my stare on the empty road ahead. "I found out after I found you with Kate."

"And you didn't think to tell me you were pregnant?"

"I was upset."

"Who went with you?"

I frown, bringing my eyes to his. "Huh?"

"For the abortion, who took you? Who looked after you?"

My mouth opens and closes a few times before I say, "I didn't get an abortion."

His frown deepens. "You don't have a kid. I've been to your house. Did you give it up?"

"Sort of."

"You're not making sense, Gemma," he barks. "Where's the kid now? Is it a boy or girl?"

"Girl," I say with a small smile. "She's at my place."

He pauses, staring at me while he gathers his thoughts. "Why are you telling me this?"

"I thought you should know."

He slams his hand against the dashboard, and I wince, jumping in fright. "Why now?"

"Because . . ."

"To pull me back in, is that it?" he spits.

"No . . . I just . . ."

"You think I'll come crawling back for a kid I don't even know?"

"I know it's a shock," I try, but he slams his hand down again.

"Stay the fuck away from me. Both of you." He gets out the car and slams the door.

I watch him stalk across the carpark as tears slip down my face. And then a rush of anger rips through me, and I dive from the car and rush after him, shoving him hard in the back and causing him to stumble a few steps.

"How fucking dare you dismiss me like I'm a piece of shit?" I scream. "Our daughter found out the truth and begged me to tell you because she wants to get to know you. Fuck knows why because you're a complete prick." He stares down at the ground with his hands on his hips. "She didn't know about either of us, but the truth came out and now she knows. She thought you deserved to know. I told her it would be pointless because you're not good enough to be in her life."

He gives a slight nod. "Glad you got that off your chest. Go home, Gemma, and don't come back here again."

I sigh heavily. "Whatever, Fletch. Good fucking riddance."

Ruby looks at me eagerly when I walk in. I shake my head slightly, and her smile fades. I hate I'm breaking her heart all over again. "I always wanted you," I tell her, shrugging out of my coat and laying it over the back of the couch. "My father was so angry because he thought I'd thrown my life away. He would have had me get rid of you completely, only I didn't find out until quite late on, so the pregnancy was too far gone for the procedure."

Sadness fills me when I think back to those days, and I lower onto the couch beside her. "I didn't have my mum around when I was small, so it was just me and him. He was already so full of anger and hate, and then he met Sarah. She couldn't have children but so badly wanted them. I don't know why because she's spent most of her time being unhappy, even when I gave her what she wanted."

"Did you have a good upbringing?" she asks, and I notice a trail of tears on her cheeks. I shake my head. "So, why would you think they'd give me a nice childhood?"

"Because he made me think they would," I explain. "He listed all the things I was shit at," I whisper. "Told me how I'd be a terrible parent because I couldn't support you. And he was right, I had nothing."

"You had me," she screams.

A sob escapes me. "He made it sound so believable. And then he offered to raise you and said it would be better that way because I'd still get to see you. The alternative was to put you up for adoption and then I'd never get to see you again. I couldn't handle that."

"There was another option. You could've just raised me."

"How?" I ask. "I was eighteen and terrified. I'd left

college and my father sent me away for the duration of the pregnancy. I lived with his sister, my disapproving aunt, and she only added to the doubt in my mind that I wouldn't cope. And when I returned, I threw myself into a career in the police force. I couldn't stand to be around Sarah while she showed you off to her friends. She even wore a fake bump." I scoff. "God, it all sounds so mad now."

"Tell me about my father," she whispers.

I stare into my lap, where my fingers are knotting together with nerves. "It's Fletch," I mutter. "You met him here that night."

She pushes to stand. "He's my father?"

I nod, and she starts to pace. "Holy shit. You've been dating him?"

"Not dating," I snap. "We met up again and we've been catching up."

"But you failed to mention me. No wonder he's pissed. I bet he's in shock."

I slowly shake my head, not wanting to give her any hope. "Fletch doesn't want kids. He never wanted them. He's a biker. He lives for his club and nothing else."

# CHAPTER 14

### Fletch

A kid. I have a kid. I groan and knock a fourth whiskey back. "Enforcer, there's a visitor," Grizz shouts from the doorway.

"I ain't taking visitors," I snap.

"Do I look like your fucking secretary?" he barks. "Deal with it yourself."

I sigh heavily and step out the clubhouse. As I get closer to the gates, I see Gemma's sister and I groan. "If you've come to talk on her behalf, I'm not interested," I snap.

"I haven't," she rushes to say. "Gemma doesn't know I'm here."

I roll my eyes. I can't be mean to a kid. "Open the gate," I tell Smoke as I pull out my phone and send a text to Gemma.

> Me: Your kid sister is at the clubhouse. Come and get her now.

"Where's Gemma?" I ask her as we head inside.

"Working."

I show her over to the couch, and she sits. I sit opposite her. "So, what brings you here?"

"She said you didn't want to know me."

I frown. "Huh?"

Her eyes widen. "Oh god, she did tell you, right? She said she told you." She buries her face in her hands. "Shit. Now, I look crazy."

"You're Gemma's sister," I say slowly. "Right?" She looks up and shakes her head. My fuzzy brain takes a few beats to catch up as I stare her down. "But you're not . . . you can't be . . ."

"Your daughter," she says quietly. "I'm your daughter."

The whiskey is making my head spin, and with this news on top, I need to lie down. I lean back on the couch and stare at the ceiling. *Fuck.*

"I know it's a shock. I'm shocked too, but right now, we're kind of in the same boat, so I thought we could at least talk."

"Yeah, I don't really do that kind of talking shit," I mumble.

"Well, listen instead," she says, suddenly sounding unsure. "I love Gemma. She's always been the best big sister. She's my safe place when my parents . . ." her voice trails off. "When Mark and Sarah were being dicks."

"Language," I mutter absentmindedly.

She gives a small laugh. "You sound just like Gem. My point is, I'm heartbroken she lied, and I suspect you are too, but she thought it was for the best. That's what everyone around her told her, and she believed them. Mark is an awful man. He treats us both like an inconvenience. But now I know the truth, I'm kind of relieved."

"Good for you."

"And you should be too."

"And why's that?"

"Because now you know the truth, you can get to know me and see I'm not so bad."

I instantly feel guilty and sit up slightly so I can look at her. She looks like Gemma. They have the same dark hair and blue eyes. "It's not because I think you're bad," I mutter.

"Then what is it?"

"I just . . . I don't want kids."

"Tough," she says with a shrug. "I'm already here."

"I won't be a good dad," I tell her honestly. "I don't even know how to do that sort of thing."

She rolls her eyes. "And I probably won't be a good daughter some of the time. We can learn together."

"Fuck, you're stubborn just like me."

"Can't we just give it a try? Together?"

We stare at one another for a solid minute. There's a million thoughts going through my mind, and then the door opens and Gemma storms in. "Ruby," she hisses, "what are you doing here?"

"I came to talk to Fletch," she says, standing. "But I'm done."

"I asked you to leave it," Gemma snaps. She turns her sad eyes on me, and I almost crack. "I'm so sorry about this. We'll leave."

"It's fine," I say. "She can stick around for a bit."

Ruby smiles wide. "We have a deal?" I nod, and she laughs. "Good."

"Not good," says Gemma. "You can't just hang around here. We'll make proper arrangements."

"I'll be fine," says Ruby. "Go back to work."

"No," snaps Gemma. "You can't stay in a biker club."

"And why's that?" I ask, arching a brow. "Bikers are suddenly not good enough in your eyes?"

"I'm responsible for her, Fletch. This is a biker club. Do you want her around criminals and sex workers?"

I scoff. "Wow. Now, you're showing your true colours."

"It's not the place for a teenager."

"Or a copper," I spit, "so leave."

"Ruby, let's go." Gemma heads for the door, but Ruby stays rooted to the spot. I smirk when Gemma looks back to find her not moving. "Ruby?"

"I want to stay a while longer, Gemma. I want to get to know him. You owe me after everything."

I see in her eyes she's going to drop it and leave. Ruby gives me a subtle smile, and Gemma rolls her eyes and stomps back out.

Once she's gone, we talk and it's surprisingly easy. She tells me about her childhood and how it was hard but not unbearable. She speaks of Gemma a lot, and how she's been her biggest cheerleader. Now, it all makes sense. But most of all, she talks about how, up until now, she's always felt something was missing, and so maybe deep down, she knew.

When Axel steps from his office with Grizz, he comes over. "She a little young?" he asks, concern lacing his words.

"It's not what you think, Pres," I mutter, standing. "She's Gemma's . . . erm, she's mine and Gemma's daughter."

Both men stare wide-eyed with shock. "Are you shitting me?" asks Grizz, looking back and forth between us. "You have a kid with the copper?"

"I just found out today."

"And now, she's here," says Axel slowly. "Did you check her for a wire?"

"Of course not," I snap. "She's just a kid. Look, it's complicated. I'll explain later."

"Or we can go to the office, and you can put my mind to rest," he insists, stepping to one side. "Grizz, go find a babysitter. In fact, get Lexi. She can sniff out a lie."

### Gemma

My mind is full of Ruby and Fletch. I can't concentrate on work, so when I get called into my father's office, it's a welcome relief from the piles of paperwork I have on my desk.

"I assume this is about Operation Sapphire?" I ask as I sit down. I've been waiting for him to tell me the plug's been pulled on the entire investigation.

"I think we both know that's been a huge failure."

"I put my report in with Karen. I tried everything and followed all the right procedures. You can't pin the failure on me." I already know the book stops with my father—he gave the go-ahead for the operation, and he cleared every raid and stop and search.

"Actually, that's not entirely true, is it, Gemma?"

I shrug. "I put it all in my statement. I can't help that the club was clean."

"This is off the record," he warns, and I sit straighter.

He never gives me inside information, so I'm intrigued. "They found a tape at the clubhouse. It was in the safe."

"Okay."

"And although I've not seen it personally, I've been told you're on it."

My blood runs cold and the visits to the clubhouse and garage race through my mind. I wasn't exactly careful sometimes. "I had my car done at the garage," I say, "but Karen knows that."

"It's not that."

"And I went to The Bar on a hen night before I knew they owned it."

"Gemma, you were recorded without your knowledge."

"Okay."

"With him," he spits, and I allow the words to sink in. "Karen is waiting for you in her office."

I push to stand on unsteady feet. I feel like my entire body is shaking as sickness swirls in my stomach. He must be wrong. Fletch wouldn't do that. *He wouldn't.*

I don't know how the hell I made it to Karen's office, but as I knock on her door, I feel weak enough to collapse. I try to remember the times I've been with Fletch and work out what he could possibly have recorded. "Come in," Karen orders, breaking me from my thoughts.

She straightens when I enter, and I see the disgust in her eyes as I take a seat.

"You've spoken with your father?" I nod. "Were you aware of the footage?" she asks coldly, and I shake my head. "Fuck, Gemma, what were you thinking?" she hisses.

"Where was it?"

"The sex or the fucking recording?"

I want to vomit. *He recorded us having sex.* "Recording," I whisper, fighting the urge to retch.

"In the safe, which the president helpfully pointed the officers to."

Tears build in my eyes, and I angrily swipe them away. "What happens now?"

"It's out of my hands. Another force is on the way to take over the case. They'll check everything, every phone call, every text message, to see if you messed up the investigation."

"I texted—" I begin to say, but she cuts me off.

"Don't tell me. Save it."

"Can I see it?" I whisper.

She sighs and shakes her head. "It's in evidence."

I groan, wondering who the hell would have watched it in the station. "What will happen to me?"

"At the very least, you'll get the sack."

"Everything was aboveboard," I whisper, "except one text."

"You told me you weren't like Lexi Cooper. You said she was a rookie and you knew better."

"We had history," I mutter.

"I don't give a shit," she screams. "And now, the entire force will be looked into."

"I'm sorry."

"If I were you, I'd get rid of the phone."

"Won't that look worse?" I sniffle.

"Worse than whatever that text was? Probably not."

I GO to the bathroom to clean myself up. The other force had arrived to interview me right as I left Karen's office.

Sitting on the toilet, I open my phone to text Ruby.

> Me: Something came up at work. Have you got your key to let yourself in at home? xx

She replies right away.

> Ruby: Yes. See you when you get back xx

Seeing the kisses at the end of her text makes me sob harder. Maybe seeing Fletch has helped her forgive me slightly.

> Me: I won't have my phone on me so if you need me urgently, call the station. xx

I stand and lift the back off the toilet system. I turn off my phone, drop it into a clear evidence bag, and place it in the water. Then I step from the cubicle, rinse my tear-stained face, and go back to Karen's office, where two men in suits are waiting for me.

## Fletch

I CHECK MY WATCH. It's late as Ruby stands to leave. "I'll walk you back," I offer. "I've had a drink, so I can't take you on the bike."

She smiles, hooking her arm in mine. "Thanks."

It feels good. She's a nice kid, and she handled the

brothers really well today. It's almost like she was cut out for club life.

As we leave, the brothers each say goodbye, and I'm filled with pride as we head out. This morning, my life felt empty and messy, but now, there's hope. Maybe I can be what Ruby needs, and it's not like she's asking for anything from me, just to get to know me.

We walk in silence the entire way, but it's comfortable. Maybe we've spoken so much, we're out of words. We slow as we reach Gemma's house. "Today was lovely," she says. "Thank you."

"It was," I agree. "Thanks for not taking no for an answer."

She laughs. "I think we've already established who I take after for stubbornness."

I look past her towards the house and make out a figure hunched over on the doorstep. I pull Ruby behind me in alarm and move closer, soon realising it's Gemma. I stop at her feet, and she finally looks up. Her eyes are swollen and red. She's been crying.

She pushes to stand, wiping her nose on her sleeve. "I forgot my key," she tells Ruby.

"Why didn't you call?" asks Ruby, producing her key. "How long have you been out here?"

Gemma avoids my curious stare, forcing a smile. "It's fine. I told you, I didn't have my phone. Are you okay?" she asks, sounding hopeful.

"I'm fine, but if you're asking if I've forgiven you, then no." Ruby unlocks the door. "Thanks for today, Fletch. I'll call you."

I give a nod, and she goes inside, leaving me and

Gemma alone. Gemma sniffles, wiping her wet cheeks as she stares after Ruby. "Are you okay?" I ask.

She brings her eyes back to me and stares for the longest time with a range of emotions passing over her face. "Goodnight," she whispers, going to walk inside. I frown, confused by her weird behaviour, and I grab her wrist to stop her. She slowly turns back to face me. "Spend the next few days getting to know Ruby, cos next week, we're moving away."

"What?"

"I lost my job," she announces, and my heart stutters. "But I guess you already knew that part."

"Snap, I—"

She rips her wrist from my grasp. "Don't fucking call me that."

I take a few steps back. "It wasn't personal," I mutter.

She scoffs, then marches towards me, rearing her hand back. I catch it before she hits my face and twist her away from me so her back is to my front. I hold her against me, despite her fighting to break free. "You've ruined my life," she cries angrily. "I didn't do anything to you to deserve this."

"That's not true, is it, Gemma? You lied . . . for years."

"You only just found out about that," she spits. "That video was with the police for days. Everyone has viewed it." She sobs harder. "They all know."

"You came for the club," I tell her, fighting the guilt. "You were never going to win."

She leans her head back against my chest and cries. Her body shakes uncontrollably. "Was it all a lie?"

I contemplate being honest, telling her how I love her more now than I did back then and how walking away is killing me. But even if I confessed now, it's all too late. Too much has happened, and I've hurt her again, so I deal the final blow while forcing myself to hold my head high. "Yes."

I release her, and she drops down, burying her face in her hands. I watch her shoulders shake from her silent tears and take a few more steps away. I did it before and I can do it again. Gemma Stone is too good for me.

She always was and she always will be.

# CHAPTER 15

**Gemma**

I don't know why it cuts so deep. Maybe it's because it's him. Maybe it's because I've let him do this to me twice now. Or maybe it's because I feel so humiliated. Either way, I've not left my bed for three days straight, and I don't feel proud. I was a fool to think I could go in there and pretend to like him enough to make him open up. When has Cameron Fletcher ever opened up about anything? After all this time and a child together, I still don't even know who his parents are.

The door opens slightly, and Ruby pops her head in. "How are you?" she asks in a soft voice. She gave up ignoring me two days ago. It's pretty hard to ignore someone who isn't even talking.

"What day is it?" I whisper.

"It's Friday. You have to go into work today, remember?"

I shake my head. That's the last place I need to go. Ruby steps in farther. "Please get up today, Gem. Shower, brush your hair. You'll feel better."

"I can't."

"You can. Just one step at a time."

I turn over so my back's to her. I hate being like this. She deserves better, but right now, I can't face anything.

---

THE DOOR OPENS, letting light into the room. I blink, trying to focus as the figure comes into view. My father glares at me with disdain. "You're just going to fester in here, are you?"

"It worked for Sarah," I mutter.

"Get up."

"No."

"Gemma, get up now or I'll drag you from that bed myself."

"You said you'd be nice," whispers Ruby. "She needs a doctor."

"She needs to wake the hell up and face up to the situation she's caused."

"She's not well."

"I'm right here," I snap, pissed they're speaking about me like I'm invisible. "I just need a few days."

"You've had a few days," Ruby argues. "I'm worried about you."

"Maybe you should go home," I admit. "I can't look after you right now."

She stares at me with eyes full of hurt, but I look away. I don't need her judgement too.

## Fletch

"You look sad," I note as Ruby stares ahead, not bothering to touch her breakfast.

"It's Gemma," she whispers with a sadness in her voice. We've avoided the topic so far, mainly because I change it whenever Gemma comes up. "She's unwell."

"What's wrong with her?" I ask, shovelling eggs into my mouth.

"She's not gotten out of bed all week."

"She'll be fine, Ruby. Sometimes adults just need time to process."

"And sometimes they need to see a doctor, but I can't even get her to shower let alone leave her room."

I drop my fork on the plate with a clatter. "Who's looking after you?"

"Me," she says with a laugh. "I always take care of myself."

"That's not on you. She should be keeping an eye on you. Have you been eating?"

"Yes, Fletch, I can cook for myself." She adds a laugh, and it just reminds me of how much I don't know about her.

"That's not the point," I snap. I spent my childhood looking after myself, and I won't let Ruby do the same. "I'll talk to her."

"No, it's fine. I think you'll make it worse."

"Worse than it already is?"

She shrugs. "Good point. She told Mark that she's planning on moving away with me."

"That ain't happening." I've spent every day this week getting to know Ruby, and no one is taking her away again. "Besides, she can't do much when she won't leave her room."

"Mark said she can't leave until her job has finished their investigation. Do you know what they're investigating?" she asks.

I shake my head. My first lie. "Stay here, give me your key. I'll go and see her."

She reluctantly hands over her key. "Please don't make it worse."

### Gemma

I GASP, sitting upright and coughing violently. "Get the fuck up." Cold water soaks into my pyjamas and bed sheets. I look up in shock to find Fletch glaring at me with an empty bucket in his hand. My heart slams hard in my chest. I grab the wet sheets and lie back down, pulling them over myself.

"Ruby is going out of her mind with worry," he yells. "Sort yourself out."

"Leave," I whisper.

"Gemma, please."

"I can't be around you," I mutter, realising how true that statement is.

"Until you start looking after Ruby, I'll be here."

"Please," I murmur, embarrassed at how desperate my voice sounds. "Just leave."

"What do you want, Gemma?" he snaps. "What's the plan here? To live in your bed forever? The problems won't go away."

"Trust me, I know."

"So, face them. Stop hiding."

"I'm not hiding."

"You're not facing them."

"I'm done," I tell him, letting my tears mix with the wetness on my pillow. "I just want to go."

"Go where?" he asks, frowning. "You're not leaving with Ruby. She's staying."

I offer a weak smile. "Ruby can't come where I want to go."

It dawns on him what I'm talking about. "Are you shitting me?" he barks. "You're better than that."

I want to hit him for that one stupid statement. If only he knew the thought I'd put into ending my life. It's not an easy decision, but I can't see a way out. "Leave."

"How can I fucking leave now you've said that?" he spits angrily.

"I'm not your problem."

"But Ruby is. Fuck, Gemma, these things are temporary, they'll go away. You have a life to live, and you want to throw it away because of a job you fucking hated anyway and a man who's not even worth a single tear?"

I begin to shiver as the cold bleeds into the bedding. I close my eyes. I'm so tired despite constantly flitting in and out of sleep. The smallest interaction makes me sleepy. I smile to myself. When I wake, he'll be gone. I *need* him to be gone.

### Fletch

I CALL AXEL. "WHAT?"

"I have a problem," I tell him. "Gemma is unwell."

"So?"

"Because of what we did to her. She wants to . . ." I

can't even bring myself to say the words. I sigh heavily. "She wants to kill herself. She hasn't left her bed in a week, and fuck knows if she's even eaten or drank a thing."

"Why are you calling me, Fletch? Do you want my permission?"

I frown in confusion. "What are you talking about?"

"You love her, and you need me to tell you to get her well again. You want my permission to be at her side right now?"

"No," I mutter. "I mean, I'm staying here until I'm certain she won't do anything crazy. But she's Ruby's mum. Ruby can't lose three parents in such a short space of time."

"I don't think Ruby is your main concern here. Why don't you just admit it? You love her."

"It doesn't matter, Pres. I made my choice."

"She isn't a copper anymore," he states.

"So?"

"And she didn't actually find anything on us."

"What are you saying?"

"Just that if you need time to make shit right with her, I'll get the garage covered."

"It's not like that," I tell him. "She just needs to get better."

He chuckles. "I'll have someone walk Ruby home."

"Thanks."

I go back into Gemma and wonder how the hell she can sleep when she's piss-wet through. I head into her bathroom and put the plug in the bath. I search the cupboard and find bath foam and some scissors. Turning the taps on full, I pour the foam into the tub and give it a swirl. I wait until it's almost full and check the temperature.

Going back into Gemma, I shrug from my kutte and place it on the chair. Then I go over to the bed and carefully pull the sheets back. She doesn't even stir as I carefully take the hem of her shirt and begin to cut a straight line from the bottom to the top. She's not wearing underwear, so I pull the shirt closed and slide my hands beneath her, lifting her into my arms. She stirs, groaning, and then rests her head against my chest, settling into my arms.

I carry her to the bathroom and carefully lower her into the bubbly water. Her eyes shoot open, and she gasps in surprise, looking alarmed as she takes in her surroundings. I pull the shirt from her arms and dump it in the sink. "Morning," I say cheerfully. "Bathtime." She grips the sides and starts to push up, but I tug her hands away so she slips back into the water, some of it spilling out over the sides. "You're having a bath."

"Why are you here still?" I hate the hurt in her eyes as she spits those words. She hates me. She can't even stand to look at me.

"I told you, I can't leave you after what you said."

"Why?" she yells. "You hate me anyway, so what difference does it make to you if I die?"

"I don't hate you, Gem."

She wraps her arms around her shoulders and rests her chin on her knees. "Of course, you do. Why else would you do what you did?"

I grab a jug and scoop some water into it. I try to wet her hair, but she moves her head to one side. I sigh heavily, taking her hair in my fist and tugging her head back. I try again, this time, wetting her hair. "When I was eight, I would wash my mother's hair." Gemma remains quiet, her eyes staring up at me as I scoop up another jug and carefully pour it over her head. "She was so depressed and strung-out on meds that didn't ever really work, she couldn't do it herself. I'd run the bath, take her by the hand and lead her to it, and once she was in, I'd wash her hair."

I smile at the memory. "She wasn't always that way. Some days, she'd seem fine. She'd be over the top and loud, spinning me around and waking me at midnight to bake a cake. But there was never an even keel with her. She was either really, really high or super low." My smile fades. "She was diagnosed bipolar, but the doctors couldn't get her medication right. She met this guy at some kind of mental health clinic. Before I knew it, she was self-medicating with his help, and he'd be the one running her baths, but not because he cared." I give my head a small, sad shake. "His friends would give him more drugs if she was clean when he passed her around."

Gemma doesn't speak as I pour shampoo into my hand and begin to rub it into her hair. She closes her eyes. "Neighbours noticed I was playing in the garden at stupid times of the night and day and reported it to the social. I was taken from her and placed into a home. I soon learned how to survive alone."

I rinse her hair and run conditioner through, and once that's rinsed, I hand her a bar of soap. "Shout if you need me." I take the scissors and notice the way she stares at them longingly. "I'll be right outside."

Ruby arrives two minutes later, rushing upstairs, her expression full of worry. "Is she okay?" She pants like she's run a marathon.

I nod, tucking her hair behind her ear. It's the first time

I've made a move to touch her, yet it feels so normal. She smiles, leaning her cheek into my palm. "You didn't yell at her?"

I smirk. "Can you strip her bed? Is there a spare room she can stay in while hers dries out?"

"Oh lord, what did you do?" Before I can answer, she rolls her eyes. "Yes. Just there," she tells me, pointing to another door. "I'll make up a new bed."

Gemma is staring straight ahead when I go back into the bathroom. She startles as I grab a towel and hold it open. "Ruby is home," I tell her. "Try for her."

She stands, and I watch the water running down her body. She's lost weight, and I hate that's because of me. As she steps out, I wrap the towel around her. She takes it, stepping from my arms, and stares down at the floor. "Ruby is making the spare bed up." She leaves the bathroom without a word and goes into the spare room without a fuss.

Ruby smiles. "It's great to see you up and about. Shall I make you some pasta?"

"No."

"You need to eat," I cut in.

She ignores me, keeping her back to me. Ruby gives me a small smile and follows me from the room, closing the door gently. "Thanks for looking after her. And for trying."

"I'm not going anywhere, Ruby," I tell her. "Not until she's better."

Relief floods her face, and it breaks my heart that she thought she'd have to deal with this shitshow alone. "We'll order Chinese, and Gemma will sit downstairs with us, even if she doesn't eat."

She begins to shake her head. "I don't think she'll come downstairs."

I grin. "Go and find a menu, we'll join you in a sec."

Once she's gone, I open the door, and Gemma is already lying under the sheets. Her eyes open and narrow when she spots me. "You'll sit with us while we eat."

"Jesus, take a hint. I don't want you here."

"Will you walk or should I carry you?"

"Don't think about touching me again."

I smile. "Great, walk it is." I wait for a beat, and when she doesn't move, I sigh. "Fine." I rip the sheets from her and discover she's still naked. I go back to her room and pull open a drawer. On top of her clothes is my shirt, the one I left here before. I take it, go back into her, and throw it at her. "Put this on or I'll carry you naked."

She growls, tugging it on and standing. "I can walk."

### Gemma

THE SMELL of the Chinese food makes my stomach growl, but whenever I think about eating, I get the urge to vomit. Fletch and Ruby chat like they've known each other for years, and I can't deny it pisses me off. She only started speaking to me because she was worried. She's treating him like her long-lost hero, and seeing them so comfortable around one another makes me wonder what I've missed out on.

"You hungry yet?" asks Fletch, and I shake my head. "Drink the water," he repeats, and I stare at the pint of water he placed in front of me ten minutes ago.

"I'm not a child."

He ignores me, turning back to Ruby and asking her about school. I snatch the glass up and take a few gulps. I don't know why I want him to approve because I fucking hate him, but when he offers a smile my way, I almost return it. Like in the bathroom when he called me 'Gem'. After him being so cold, hearing that affectionate name fall from his lips made me swoon. I wanted to hear it again, and I hate that I'm so damn weak for him.

Ruby finishes her dinner and places her plate in the sink. "I have homework," she says in an almost apologetic tone.

"It's fine. We're good here," Fletch tells her, and she disappears.

"Water," he tells me again. "All of it."

"Why did you tell me about your mum?" I ask.

"If you want me to answer questions, Gem, you gotta drink more water." There it is again, that piece of affection. I drink more water, draining half the glass. "Good girl," he whispers, and something inside me sits taller under his praise. *Fuck, I'm an idiot.*

"I don't want Ruby to feel like I did. I don't want her to end up in care."

"She wouldn't," I whisper, frowning.

"Really? Who's on her birth certificate?"

I stare down at the table. "Sarah and my father."

"So, we have no parental rights. And your father is pissed at you, so who would stop her being taken into care? You have to fix up, Gemma."

"I will," I mutter. "You can check in daily if you don't believe me."

He smirks. "I'm not leaving until I know for certain you're not going to do anything stupid."

I scoff. "I already did that—I met you. I'm fine. Ruby will update you anyway."

He shakes his head. "I'm staying."

"Please, Fletch. I don't think having you here is going to make me better."

"I'm staying." His tone is so final, I give up and sit in silence while he begins to clear the plates away.

# CHAPTER 16
**Fletch**

When I go in to check on Ruby, she's fast asleep. I turn off her bedside light, musing at how quickly I've stepped into a role I thought I never wanted. She makes it all so easy, and liking her isn't a choice when her presence is so infectious.

Gemma is staring up at the ceiling when I go in, then I feel her eyes on me. "What are you doing?" she asks when I drop into the reclining chair.

"Sleeping."

"There's a perfectly good couch. Or better still, go home."

"I can't leave you alone."

"Why?"

"You know why, Snap. Now, go to sleep."

"How can I when you're right there watching me?"

I grin. "You slept in a wet bed earlier. Close your eyes and just sleep."

She growls in annoyance and rolls over, wrapping the sheets around her tightly. "I hate you."

"No, you don't."

---

I wake with a start in time to see Gemma leaving the bedroom. I scramble to my feet, rushing after her. "What's going on?" I ask, catching her wrist before she manages to descend the stairs. She's dressed, and when she turns to look at me, she's applied makeup. I frown at the sudden turnaround in her attitude.

"I have to go in to work and face my bosses."

"I don't know if that's a good idea," I say, allowing her to head downstairs with me following.

"I've already put them off enough."

"Yesterday, you didn't want to get out of bed, and now, you're floating down the stairs like the ghost of Christmas past. You haven't eaten in days. At least let me fix you some breakfast." I watch as she pushes her feet into heels.

Ruby comes down the stairs rubbing the sleep from her eyes. "What's going on?"

"Your mum," I hear Gemma's sharp intake of breath but continue anyway, "thinks she's ready to face her bosses."

"Christ," says Ruby, "I don't think that's a good idea."

"That's exactly what I said," I tell her.

"I'm fine," says Gemma, grabbing her bag. "I told you, I just needed a few days to sort my head out." She unlocks the door. "And when I get back, I want you gone, Fletch." She leaves, slamming the door.

I stare at it for a few seconds before turning to Ruby. "You think she's okay?"

She shakes her head. "Nope."

"Do you think she meant it when she said she wants me gone?"

Ruby smirks. "Oh yeah."

"Nah, she was bluffing," I say with a shrug.

"What are you gonna do?"

I head for the kitchen. "Make breakfast and wait for her to return."

"I don't think she'll be happy when she sees you're still here."

"I'm counting on it."

We eat breakfast and talk about Ruby's friends. I like hearing about her life, even though she tells me about a few boys in her friendship circle. The feeling in my chest isn't like anything I've ever felt. I know how boys' minds work and I hate that she's so young and naïve to it.

Once she's gone for her shower, I put a call in to Nyx.

"Hey, brother, when you coming home?"

I grin. "Are you missing me?"

He laughs. "Nah, I'm getting all the club pussy, it's great. But seriously, what's going on?"

"Gemma seemed fine today. It's a stark comparison to yesterday. I think she's putting on a front so I'll leave her alone."

"And are you gonna?"

"Nah. I don't trust her after what she said."

"Pres called church last night, said you were in love with Gemma."

"He did what?" I snap, pissed he went behind my back.

"Relax. He wanted to make sure we were all okay with it."

It piques my interest. "And were you all okay?"

He laughs again. "You know no one goes against the Pres, brother. He laid your case out, and he's right, she didn't get nothing on the club and there's history between you. You got a kid, so we gotta accept your decision."

"Thanks, man, I needed to hear that."

"Plus, I get to keep all the women to myself now."

### Gemma

Karen smiles, but it's not her usual bright smile. It's an awkward sort, like she doesn't know what to say to me. And beside her is my father.

"I imagine this is as awkward for you as it is for us," Karen says. "So, basically, we would like to make you a deal."

I sit straighter. "Hand in your notice with immediate effect," my father cuts in, "and there will be no investigation."

I suspected he'd want this brushed under the carpet without the scandal tainting his reputation. "Just like that?"

"Yes, Gemma," he says sternly. "Do you really want the entire team dragged through a hearing? They'll ask all kinds of questions that will paint you in a very bad light."

"I thought you'd at least offer me a transfer," I spit.

He laughs, and it's cold and empty. "You're lucky this isn't going further."

"You mean you are," I snap, pushing to stand. "This is what you've wanted all along, for me to leave the force."

"Let's just calm down," whispers Karen. "This is the best way to deal with it, Gemma. If we have to take this public, it will look bad on all of us, you included. You're a fantastic officer, and we'll be sad to see you go. I expect your resignation by the end of the day."

I roll my eyes, pulling out the letter I'd already written because I knew this would be how it would end. I slam it on the table and leave.

My father catches me in the hall. "Gemma," he hisses until I stop and turn to face him. He glances around nervously. "This is about protecting us both. It's not personal."

"Bullshit. I've done what you've asked. Now, I want something from you. I want you to legally sign Ruby over to me."

"What?"

"You heard. She's my daughter. I want to be on her birth certificate."

"Gemma, that's impossible. We lied. We can't just change it."

"Find a way."

### Fletch

GEMMA STEPS into the kitchen and stares at me. "I thought I asked you to leave."

"I told you I'm staying until you're well again."

She dumps her bag on the side and kicks off her heels. "I lost my job today," she tells me, heading to the fridge. I watch in silence as she pulls out a bottle of white wine then goes to the cupboard and pulls out a large glass. "Years of hard work gone because I made a stupid mistake with you . . . again."

"I'm sorry," I mutter.

She unscrews the cap and pours the wine until the glass is almost overflowing, then she slams the bottle down and takes a few large gulps. "That's it?" she asks. "You're sorry?"

"Look, don't fucking pretend I'm the bad guy here. You were trying to set me up too. You thought I'd be an easy way in." She rolls her eyes and drinks some more. "You wouldn't have continued seeing me if you weren't so obsessed with the club."

"You recorded me having sex," she cries, slamming the glass down and spilling some of the wine onto the table. "You *are* the bad guy, Fletch."

"I did what I had to do to protect the club."

"Of course, you did, because that means more to you than anything, right?"

"Yes," I snap. "Yes, it does."

"So, what about Ruby?" she screams. "Where will she come into it all, because you've already proved you'll put that gang first."

It's blind rage that has me moving fast until I have her against the wall. "She's different," I growl, pushing my forehead to hers. "And I'm not in a gang." She's not scared. She hardly even bats an eyelid as I cup her jaw and stare her down. "You're standing here like you're the injured party, yet I'm the one who's been lied to for all these years."

"I'm taking Ruby away from here," she says firmly.

"Not a chance," I spit, pushing away from her and turning my back so I can gain control of the anger swirling inside me. "I've only just found her. You're not taking her anywhere."

"You can't stop me."

"Like fuck I can't. What your parents did was illegal," I tell her, "but I'm sure you already know that. You try to take her away and I'll call the police and the social and tell them how your father lied."

"Do you think I care what happens to them?" she asks, laughing. It's cold and empty. "I can't stay here. I can't be around you."

"It's not about you, Gemma. Ruby wants to get to know me. And I . . . I want to get to know her too."

"Did you all laugh?" she asks, her voice low as she stares down at the floor. "Did you watch that footage and laugh?"

"No."

When her eyes reach mine, I see the hurt all over again. "Did you watch it?"

I shake my head. "No. Nobody did."

"I don't believe you," she whispers. "I thought it hurt the first time when you left me, but this . . . this is so much worse. I feel betrayed, Fletch."

"And you don't think I feel exactly the same, Gemma?" I snap. "I have a fucking daughter. She's practically grown, and I knew nothing about her. I didn't watch her grow or hear her first words. You betrayed me, so I ain't gonna feel bad for protecting my club from you. Stop playing the victim when you're just as bad."

She goes to grab the glass, but I swipe it away, sending it across the room. It smashes and she stares at the wine now running down the wall. "You need to fucking eat something," I spit, storming out the room.

## Gemma

I sit at the kitchen table staring into space. I'm hurt but Fletch is too. Somehow that pisses me off more. He's done so much to me, yet he still throws everything back on me. I lied. It was huge, I get that, but I've tried to explain why I couldn't tell him about Ruby. Fuck, I've spent most of my adult life regretting that decision to let my father take her from me.

I push my chair back and head upstairs, ignoring the way the two of them are together again, watching a film.

I go into my bedroom and notice the mattress is now dry. I drop to my knees and feel around under my bed until my hands land on the box. I slide it out and tuck it under my arm before heading back downstairs. I stand in front of the television until I have their attention, and Ruby uses the remote to pause it.

"I lied to you both," I say, "and I wish I hadn't. God, I wish I could change so much. But I want you both to know I didn't mean to hurt you. So . . ." I drop to my knees and place the box on the floor. I haven't looked in here for so long, I'm nervous. "I wanted to share this with you."

I lift the lid and both lean forward slightly. "I kept everything I could," I explain, pulling out a small white envelope and delving inside to retrieve the small lock of blonde hair tied neatly with a small pink ribbon. "Your first haircut," I tell Ruby, passing it over. "You were two and you hated it. You screamed the place down." I pull out the picture showing Ruby's red, tear-stained face. "The hairdresser couldn't get the fringe straight because you wouldn't sit still," I add with a laugh. They both stare at the picture. Ruby smiles, but Fletch looks sad, so I move on quickly, pulling out a scan picture. "I had to sneak these because Sarah took them. She never noticed when I stole them back."

Ruby joins me on the floor, taking everything I pass her way and studying it with a huge smile. "I made a scrapbook," I add, passing that to Fletch. He takes it, staring at the cover which has pictures of Ruby all over the front. "Of all her firsts. There're some pictures of the ones I witnessed. I even wrote her first word," I say proudly.

He dumps the scrapbook on the side and stands. "I need air," he mutters, heading out.

Ruby places her hand over mine. "He's struggling," she whispers.

"I'm trying," I mutter. "I can't change it now, but I'm trying to make it right."

"I know," she says, smiling, "and I love all this. The fact you kept it all makes me feel loved . . . Mum." It's the second time I've heard it today and it feels so foreign. Ruby winces. "Is it too weird?" I shake my head, scared to say anything in case I break down. "Cos I can stick to Gemma if you prefer, but I just thought . . . I can't call you Gemma forever."

I nod. "It's fine," I whisper. "Just feels strange."

"Go and speak to him. I'd really like to get to know you both properly, as my parents."

---

I STEP INTO THE GARDEN, where I find Fletch staring up at the sky. He gives a side glance but doesn't speak as I lower onto the wall beside him. "We're both upset for very different reasons," I begin, "and I'm trying to make it right, okay. Yes, I lied, but I can't change that now."

"That's the worst thing about it," he mutters. "You can't change it. We can't go back in time."

I sigh. "I wish I could, Fletch. I'm sorry, okay, but I was young and scared, and you left me. Not only that, you fucked my best friend."

He stares down at the ground. "Yeah, I know. I fucked up. You wanna know why I did that?" He glances at me, and I nod. "I thought I wasn't good enough." He gives an unamused laugh. "You were sneaking around to see me, and I was sick of it. Every time you cancelled because you couldn't sneak out, I got more and more pissed. She was there, flirting and telling me how lucky you were to have me but how ashamed you were. I just gave in, but I knew you'd catch us. She knew it too, and I didn't care. You caught us and ran, and it just confirmed that I wasn't good enough for you. I'd messed it up because I wasn't good enough."

"It was never you," I whisper. "I told you so many times, I was terrified he'd ruin it. And I know it ruined us anyway, but I just thought if I could reach my twenty-first, I could leave home and run away with you." I laugh. "I was young and naïve. Then I found out about the baby, and I panicked. My first love had cheated on me, and I was having his baby. Of course, my father wasted no time telling me how you'd be a terrible father, and because you'd let me down so badly already, I believed him."

"It must've been hard on you," he mutters, placing a hand over mine as it rests on my knee. I stare at it, wishing we'd never met again that night in The Bar. "Watching her grow up without her knowing the truth."

"I learned to live with it."

"Now Sarah has left, what will happen with Ruby?"

I shrug. "I asked my father to change the birth certificate. Of course, it's not that simple. It would implicate him in a crime."

Fletch stands. "Leave it to me." I watch in confusion as he leaves through the back gate.

# CHAPTER 17
**Fletch**

"You want to blackmail the Chief of Police?" Grizz repeats, smirking in Axel's direction.

"What choice do I have?" I ask.

"You could just not do it," says Axel with a laugh.

"He's right, brother, have you lost your mind?"

"What if this was Elsie?" I demand. "Wouldn't you want to be on her birth certificate?"

"It's different," he argues. "I could add mine because hers was aboveboard. How the fuck will you get Ruby's changed without causing a shitstorm?"

"The same way he did it—illegally."

"He must know someone," adds Axel thoughtfully. "If he doesn't, we do."

"First of all, are you claiming the copper?" asks Grizz.

"She's not a copper anymore," I tell him. "She quit today at their request."

"Fuck," mutters Axel. "How she take that?"

"Not great, but we have other matters to sort."

"You should know we took a vote on accepting Gemma into the club," Axel tells me.

I nod, not telling him that Nyx already filled me in. "And?"

"And if it's what you want, she's in."

I give a nod. "Okay. So, let's sort this first and I'll decide."

Grizz fist bumps me, probably relieved he can relax now I won't be looking at his old lady. "Let's go and pay him a visit."

---

"You booked us in to see him?" I ask, glaring at Axel.

He grins, nodding. "How brazen, right?"

"Or stupid," I mutter as we approach the front desk of the police station.

"We have an appointment with Mark Stone," Axel announces proudly.

The officer looks us up and down warily before picking up the telephone to inform Gemma's father of our arrival. "How did you even get us an appointment?" asks Grizz.

"I called his secretary," says Axel like it's the most normal thing in the world. "Don't tell Lexi, but we had a thing a few years back. She worked for the Chief of Police before Mark, and probably the one before him."

"Fuck, how old is his secretary?" I ask.

The officer buzzes the side door open and instructs us to come through. He meets us the other side and leads us along the corridor. An older woman stands to greet us, fixing her eyes on Axel with a small smile pulling on her glossed lips. "He'll be right out," she tells us just as the office door opens and Gemma's father glares at us.

"Step in here," he barks, and we file through like naughty schoolboys.

He slams the door and goes behind his desk. "Is this a joke?" he asks.

"You tell me," I counter. "Ruby certainly doesn't think so."

He scoffs. "That's what this is about? Ruby?"

"I want my name on the birth certificate," I tell him, and he laughs, "and Gemma's."

"Impossible."

"Find a way," I tell him firmly.

"Not a chance," he spits, glaring at me. "Now, get the hell out."

"I don't think you understand," I say, pulling out the second copy of the sex tape. He stares at it warily. "Of course, we made copies," I confirm with a smirk.

"I can see the headlines now," says Axel, staring off into space. "Chief of Police's police officer daughter in sex scandal with suspected criminals the Met were investigating."

Grizz laughs too. "Or London's Met police sleeping with the enemy."

"Good one," says Axel, and they fist bump.

"You neanderthals," spits Mark. "It's Gemma's face that will be out there."

Axel smirks. "Not just her face."

"How about, Chief of Police steals vulnerable teenage daughter's baby?" I suggest, placing my hands on the desk and fixing him with a stare. "I don't care how you do it, but you *will* change that birth certificate because we have enough shit to throw your way."

He leans back in his chair. "I did you a favour," he

says. "She had the best education, the best upbringing, all the things you could never have offered her. And now, you want to rip her away from all she's known and raise her in your clubhouse?" His laugh is mocking, and it instantly pisses me off. I clench my fist, and Axel spots it, shaking his head in my direction as a warning not to smash it into his face.

"I don't care if we shame your daughter," Axel announces, heading for the door. "She isn't our concern. But we will release that tape and everything else we know if you don't sort it by this time tomorrow."

## Gemma

My father is raging. I can hear his footsteps as he paces his office. "Is this what you want?" he yells. "To embarrass me?"

"I didn't know he was going to go to your office," I repeat.

"He doesn't care about you," he shouts, "He said as much. He's willing to send that tape to the news outlets. Everyone will see what you did."

"Then change the birth certificate," I argue.

"And then what? He'll use that tape over and over."

"He won't," I tell him. "I'll get the tape and destroy it. I don't want this out there any more than you do," I reassure him. "Just change the birth certificate."

I disconnect right as Fletch enters with Axel and Grizz. They're laughing about something, so he's too distracted to see my hand as it sails towards him, slapping his cheek so hard that my palm instantly burns.

"How fucking dare you?" I scream, not caring when he wraps a hand around my neck and forces me against the wall. His face is red with anger, and his eyes are burning into mine as Axel tries to pull him from me. "Give me the tape. Every last copy," I demand.

"Not happening," he spits, gripping my throat harder.

"You're gonna sell me out again to get what you want," I cry. Axel manages to pull Fletch from me and puts himself between us. "You're gonna ruin me again," I say, this time letting the tears flow. "You fucking wanker." I rush upstairs to my bedroom, slamming the door extra hard.

Ten minutes pass before there's a light knock on the door. "Go away."

"Will you at least let me explain?" asks Fletch. I pull the door open, and he leans on the door frame while I drop back on my bed and stare at the ceiling. "He'll change the birth certificate. The tape won't get out there."

"And if he doesn't?"

"He will."

"But if he doesn't?" I yell.

"We'll deal with that if it happens. I have other shit on him, Gem."

"Don't fucking 'Gem' me," I spit. "Not right now, when I'm so mad at you."

"You've spent half your life being mad at me," he retorts. "When will that end?"

"Maybe when you grow the fuck up."

He rolls his eyes. "Cos you're handling all of this so well."

I sit up. "I wanted to set you up," I admit. "Okay, there, I said it. When I raided your club and saw you in bed with that slapper, I thought, he hasn't changed. He's still the fuck boy who broke my heart and he deserves to suffer for putting me through everything he did. I was angry you walked away, okay, and I know you didn't know about Ruby, so I shouldn't be mad, but I am, and I can't help it. But there was also intelligence on your club, okay, and I wanted to take all the drugs off the streets. I was doing my job."

"You tried to entrap me," he states.

"Yes," I say, nodding. "But it didn't work because you were also lying. You were trying to keep me close to find out what I knew. You made me think there was something between us. We're as bad as each other."

"How do we move forward?"

"We don't."

"For Ruby," he adds.

I sigh. "We forgive each other for what we did."

He thinks over my words. "Can you move past it?"

I shrug. "Can you?"

"Maybe."

"Then let's agree to at least try."

He gives a nod and steps farther into the room. "I read your diary," he admits, and I frown. "The one in Ruby's memory box." I relax slightly. I'd kept a diary of all the things she did or said that I found funny. "I'm glad you kept all that stuff."

"Me too."

"Let's go out for dinner," he suggests. "Me, you, and Ruby."

I bite on my lower lip. I don't have to hide from the public any longer, but it still feels strange. "Okay."

Nicola Jane

---

Fletch found a nice place that catered to Ruby's specific request of a gourmet burger. And as we all sit, it feels right, like this is how it was always supposed to be, and again, I'm hit with the guilt that I let my father take her from me.

"So, what's your plan?" asks Ruby, and I arch a brow, not having a clue what she's referring to. "What will you do for work?"

"Oh." I take a drink. I haven't given it as much thought as I should have. "No idea."

"Do you have savings to help pay the bills until you find something?" asks Fletch.

I nod. "But they won't last long. Maybe I can speak to my father and ask again for a transfer?"

"For a job you never wanted to do?" asks Fletch. "You don't seem sad you lost it."

I shrug. "I don't feel sad."

"So, why continue? You didn't get your father's approval, which is why you did it."

"He's right. A career change is exactly what you need," Ruby agrees.

"I don't have any idea what else I'm good at," I argue. "I've put everything into this career."

"Take some time," suggests Fletch.

"Speaking of jobs," says Ruby, glancing at Fletch, "Dad said I could help in the garage on Saturdays . . . just in the office," she adds.

I frown at her using the term 'dad' when she's only just met Fletch. It sounds odd, but he doesn't seem to mind. In fact, he beams in delight. "You're a little young," I argue.

"Come on, Gem, a Saturday job might do her good after all that private schooling."

"What will happen with that?" asks Ruby.

Sadness hits me again. Ruby's life will change so much already, and now, she'll have to start all over again at a new school, making new friends. "I don't think Mark will continue to pay," I admit. "And I don't know if I can afford the fees."

"I'll cover it," says Fletch without missing a beat. I begin to shake my head in protest, but he holds a hand up. "She can't leave the place because of us, especially when she's got friends and a life there. I'll cover it."

"And will I stay living with you?" she asks, looking in my direction.

"Yes."

"Unless she can't get a job and cover her mortgage, then you'll stay at the clubhouse."

Ruby's eyes widen. "Oh my god, can I?"

"No," I snap, glaring at him.

"You think I'd see my daughter on the streets?"

Ruby smirks. "You guys are already arguing like real parents. It's so cool."

---

AFTER DINNER, Fletch insists we head back to the clubhouse. Ruby already loves it there, so I don't really get a say, and as we step inside, she's met by various bikers who fist bump her in greeting like she's always been a part of the club. It's sweet to see, and for a minute, I almost forget who these men are and what they're capable of.

"You shouldn't say things like that in front of Ruby," I

whisper to Fletch. "We need to discuss living arrangements before you offer promises."

He shrugs. "If you lose your house, she'll be here with me. There's nothing to discuss."

"I won't lose my house," I snap. "But even if I did, I'd sort Ruby, not you."

"Yah know, an easy solution would be you both just move in here with me."

I frown, then laugh. He doesn't join me. "You're serious?"

"Why not?"

I scoff, and my mouth opens and closes a few times, trying to think of what to say. In the end, all I can come up with is, "No."

"I missed out on so much with Ruby. I don't want to miss any more."

"Jesus, Fletch, you didn't even want kids."

"But then I discovered I had one."

"And now, you want to be father of the bloody year, paying her school fees, giving her a place to live."

He sighs. "Yah know, I'm being polite by asking. If I have to fight for her, I will, and then the offer won't be extended to you."

"Great," I mutter. "Our truce lasted a couple hours. I'm sick of men bullying me into making decisions so they get what they want."

"Hi, Gemma." I turn to find Luna smiling. "I have a surprise for you."

My frown deepens, but before I can question her, she grabs my hand and leads me outside and round to the back of the clubhouse. I stare wide-eyed at the bright flowerpots. "What's this?" I ask.

"I love flowers," she says, "and when Fletch said you wanted to open a shop before, it got me thinking about this empty space out here." She crouches down and sniffs a tulip. "I had Grizz dig over these beds for me, and today, I got all these plants."

I run my eyes over the pots and smile. "You must've spent a fortune."

"Maybe you can help me?"

"With?"

She laughs. "Planting them in the beds. It's hardly a shop's worth, but I'd love to have them in The Bar and at The Zen Den." I glance back in the direction we just came from. "What else are you doing right now, apart from arguing with Fletch?"

I give a shrug, and she hands me a set of gardening gloves. I smile, taking them. "Thanks."

"I've never seen him so serious," she tells me, grabbing some pots and moving them over to one of the empty flower beds. "He's usually a flirt or fooling around. Since you, he's been more serious."

"Great, now, I make him miserable," I mutter.

She grins. "That's not what I'm saying. I think you make him happy. He wants to be a better man for you."

"What yah doing?" We both turn at the sound of Lexi's voice.

"Planting. You want to help?" asks Luna, standing to grab another pair of gloves. She throws them to Lexi, who eyes me suspiciously as she pulls them on. "I was just telling Gemma how Fletch seems a lot more serious these days."

"He's had to suddenly grow up after finding out about his kid," she mutters, arching a judgemental brow.

"Hey," says Luna, frowning, "it's not easy to tell a brooding biker he's a dad."

"Sorry," Lexi mumbles, grabbing a small trowel.

Luna smiles at me. "I didn't tell Grizz either. Not right away."

"You didn't tell anyone you'd even had a baby," adds Lexi.

"I couldn't face the rejection," she admits, and there's a vulnerability in her eyes.

"So, what was your reason?" asks Lexi, beginning to move the dirt into a pile.

I'm not sure I'm ready to open up to these women, but something tells me I should because winning them over will help me win over Fletch. I almost laugh to myself. Why the hell do I want to win him after everything? I give my head a shake. "My father convinced me to give Ruby up. I wasn't very confident back then. I'm still not, really," I add, almost as an afterthought. "And I'd found Fletch with . . ." They stare at me, waiting. "He was with my best friend."

"Oh shit," mutters Luna, wincing.

"He's not the most loyal," adds Lexi, and I stare down at the tulips in my hand.

"Yeah, I'm starting to see that."

"He's changed," argues Luna. "You're not being fair," she adds, giving Lexi a pointed look. "I think he just struggles to open up, and until he does, he'll keep fucking up so he doesn't have to face things."

"I don't know anything about him," I admit. "He never spoke of his life when he was younger."

"Didn't he end up in care?" asks Lexi.

Luna nods. "He doesn't talk about it, not even to the guys."

I frown, remembering the file I dug up on Fletch. *What the hell did I do with it?* I make a mental note to look when I get home because I definitely had it there last.

"Well, maybe he'll open up now," says Lexi. "He seems into you."

I scoff. "He hates me, and right now, I'm not his biggest fan either. I lied about Ruby, and he set me up."

"You came for him first," says Lexi, shrugging. "All's fair in love and war, right?"

"How can you even justify what he's done?" I ask, dropping the tulips into the planter. "I've lost my job, my career."

Lexi frowns. "You knew the risks."

"But nobody would've known had he not made a tape."

"There's a tape?" asks Luna, but neither of us reply because we're both in an intense stare-off. "What's on it?"

"He had to protect the club," Lexi says.

"And what about me?" I snap. "I thought he liked me, and all along, he was playing me."

"Weren't you doing the same?" she demands. "The audacity to sit here complaining about what he did when you were doing the exact same."

"Do you even remember what it was like before the club?" I snap. "Do you remember what being a police officer stood for?"

She gives a nod. "Yes, but I also remember what it felt like to be used. They get you in and pretend you're part of the 'blue lights family' but it's bullshit. They didn't give a crap about putting me in danger."

"You could've said no."

"They should never have put me in the position they did. Look how quickly they dropped you just so they didn't have to explain the fuck-up. All they care about is their reputation."

"I wanted this time to be peaceful," mutters Luna. "Why are you arguing when you're both in the same boat? You fell in love."

I scowl. "I did not."

"We're not alike," Lexi adds, like she's disgusted to be compared to me.

I smirk. "You're right. I never broke the law for the club." She scoffs, shaking her head. "What?" I ask. "I didn't."

"Right, of course."

"I tipped him off, it's not the same."

"You still broke the law by doing that, and you carried drugs."

I stare wide-eyed. "I did not."

She grins. "Axel has a picture that says otherwise."

"What?" I gasp, pushing to stand.

"That's enough," snaps Luna. "Lexi, go inside, you're out of order."

"What picture? I didn't move drugs."

Lexi also stands, pulling off her gloves and dropping them to the ground. "Forget it." She begins to head back inside, but I rush after her.

"No, I won't forget it. What picture?"

# CHAPTER 18
### Fletch

The door swings open and Lexi storms in, followed quickly by Gemma. I groan, exchanging a wary look with Axel, who is already on his feet. "What's going on?" he demands, stepping in front of Lexi so she has no choice but to stop.

"I'm sorry," she mutters.

"You have a picture of me?" asks Gemma, but it's said more as a statement than a question.

Axel smirks. "I have several."

"I want them all right now."

A second groan escapes me because making demands of Axel won't go well. I head over. "Let's just calm down."

"Calm down? What pictures does he have of me?" Gemma yells.

Ruby follows me over. "What's she talking about?"

"Nothing. Gemma, let's go into the office and talk," I say, trying to remain calm.

"She said I moved drugs," Gemma shouts. "Get me the pictures right now."

Axel smirks. "You're lucky this idiot is thinking of claiming you." And he turns to go to the office.

"Claiming me?" she repeats, looking me up and down, reminding me exactly what she really thinks of me. I roll my eyes and head for the office too while she follows.

I close the door, leaving Ruby outside looking confused. Axel opens his drawer and throws several photographs on the desk. Gemma swipes them up and flops back into the chair, staring at the first picture of me and her in the window of her place, fucking. I have her by the hair, tugging her head back so she's looking up at the ceiling, and I'm staring right at the camera.

Gemma slowly looks to me, tears balancing on her lower lashes. "You knew he was there," she whispers, and I can hardly deny it. She moves to the next. It's similar, so she moves straight on to one of us on the bike. She's holding the black bag. Again, she brings her eyes to mine. "What was in the bag?"

"It's not important now," I mutter.

"What was in the fucking bag, Fletch?" she yells, throwing the pictures back on the desk and standing. "I swear to god, you better tell me right now."

"Drugs," says Axel simply. I glare at him, and he shrugs. "She can't do anything about it, she's holding them."

"I didn't know," she shouts angrily.

"But your boss ain't gonna believe that, is she?" he asks, smiling. "You've been lying to her for weeks. And I have a very good lawyer who'll rip you to pieces in a courtroom."

"You absolute fucking bastard," she whispers, heading for the door.

"Gem, wait," I mutter.

She pulls the door open, and Ruby's still waiting. "Are you okay?" she asks, but Gemma passes her without a word.

"Gemma, please," I call after her.

I watch her leave, then I turn back to Axel. "Why did you tell her?"

"Because she needed to know."

"I should go after her," says Ruby.

"No," I say firmly. The last thing I need is Gemma taking Ruby away, and while she's this upset, who knows what she's capable of.

My mobile rings, and I answer. "I have the papers. I'll text you a place to meet," Mark says then disconnects.

I turn to Axel. "He has the paperwork to make me and Gemma legal guardians of Ruby," I whisper. "Can you keep an eye on her while I go and get it?" He gives a nod. "I'll find Gemma after."

---

MARK CHOOSES to meet in a busy restaurant. I sit opposite him, and he slides an envelope towards me. "How is Ruby?" he asks, his eyes fixed on the window beside us.

"She's fine."

"I'm moving away," he tells me. "There's an account set up in Ruby's name. Only she can access it when she turns twenty-one." He slides another envelope towards me. "I know you think what I did was wrong, but I wanted what was best for Gemma and Ruby."

"What was best was to leave them with me in the first place."

"So you could break them both?" he sneers. "You were never good enough for Gemma, and you still aren't."

"You don't even know me," I spit. "You have no idea who I am."

He smirks. "I know a lot more than you think, Cameron Fletcher." He pushes to stand. "I can only hope Gemma and Ruby wake up before it's too late."

---

I HEAD BACK to the clubhouse, stopping at the office. Axel looks up and asks, "You get it?" I nod, holding up the envelope. "Good. Lexi set up a room on your floor for Ruby. She's gone for a lie-down."

I thank him and head upstairs. I sit on my bed and open the envelopes. The first is a birth certificate for Ruby, with mine and Gemma's names as parents. The second is the bank details for Ruby. I reach under my bed and retrieve the file I took from Gemma's. I open it and lay it on the bed, staring at the picture of myself as a child. I was a scrawny kid who needed a haircut and a good bath. I smile sadly at the picture before turning it over and picking up the social services report.

I scan the document, the worst bits standing out. *Malnourished. Scared. Unkempt. Cameron's mother explicitly asked for us to remove him from her care as she no longer feels she can give him the care he needs. When removing Cameron from the property, she made no move to say goodbye or to console him.* I shake my head. What kind of woman ignores her child when he's screaming for her because he's terrified? I slam the folder closed. I don't need to read it because I've read it a hundred times or more and the memories haunt me still.

There's a light knock on the door. "Come in," I mutter.

Ruby pokes her head in. "Did you find Gemma?"

"I haven't been out to look yet. Are you comfortable staying here tonight?"

She smiles. "Yes. I love it here." She sighs. "When you find her, please work things out. I really want you to get along." I give a slight nod. "She's not a bad person."

"I know," I say.

"She's still the girl you loved back when you were both young."

"Nah," I say, standing, "she isn't. And neither am I. But that's okay because we're older and wiser." I place an arm around her and lead her back to her room. "Stop worrying, I'll make everything right."

"If she's not at home, I know where she might be."

## Gemma

I STARE out at the fast-flowing water. It's been a while since I felt the need to sit here and enjoy the peace. I stumbled across this part of the docks when I first moved here. I was checking out a tip that led to nothing, but I noticed this abandoned barge floating here and took an hour to sit and think over my life. I've come back several times since, just to get my head straight.

I thought moving here would be better for me, but seeing how messed-up Sarah was and how neglected Ruby felt just made me feel guilty. And my father proved pretty quickly that he hadn't changed. But Peter seemed so set on staying here. He said it was perfect for his career. Now, Sarah's left, my father texted me to say he was leaving too, and Peter has moved out. Everything just fell to shit, and it started when I decided to go after that damn biker club.

I groan, pushing to stand and gripping the rusty railings to peer over the edge. The water swirls in dark, murky circles, hitting the barge and splashing back.

"Nothing's that bad, Snap."

I startle at the sound of Fletch's voice. I glance his way, and he stuffs his hands in his pockets. He almost looks as defeated as me. "How did you find me?"

"Ruby said you like to come here when things get too much." I slide back down onto my backside and dangle my legs over the edge as Fletch joins me. "I think it's time we laid our cards on the table." He pulls out the photographs I'd thrown on Axel's desk from his pocket. "I'm sorry," he says clearly, ripping the pictures right down the middle. He sprinkles them into the water, and I watch them get swept under the waves. "When I saw you again in The Bar, time stood still, and I was transported right back to when we were younger. I loved you, Gemma. More than you could ever know."

I turn to stare at him, resting my cheek on the rusty rail. "I loved you too."

"The thing is, Gem, I still love you now. I don't think I ever really stopped."

My heart stutters in my chest. The words mean something when they come out of his mouth because I know love doesn't come easily to him. "I've fucked up," he continues, "and I don't even know where to start or how to make it right, but I will . . . if you'll let me."

"So much has happened," I utter.

"I push people away," he confesses. "The second they get too close, I find an excuse to push them away. I didn't mean to hurt you again." He sighs heavily. "That's a lie—I knew I'd hurt you, but I didn't stop to think it through. I just wanted you to back off the club because . . . I know you don't understand, but they're my family, and I'd do anything to protect them."

"I know," I whisper.

"It wasn't a lie. The way I feel or anything that happened between us since you came back wasn't a lie," he tells me. "I said it to hurt you, to push you away, but everything we did was because I wanted it to happen. I love you, Gemma, and I can't lie to myself anymore."

"I thought I could make you trust me," I admit with a small smile. "I underestimated how much the club means to you."

"I've spent my life not feeling connected to anything. I was unwanted and unloved." My heart twists, and I place my hand over his. "With you, things felt good, but even you were ashamed. That abandoned house I took you to, that was my house, Gem, and you were so disgusted, I lied because I thought you'd leave if you knew the truth. I never felt good enough, and you only instilled that by sneaking around."

I go to reply, but he holds a hand up, so I clamp my mouth shut. "I get why you did that, but at the time, I felt rejected . . . again. So, I tried to let you down gently, but you wouldn't give up on me. You made excuses for my shitty behaviour, and I knew the only way out was to sleep with Kate."

"You could've just told me straight, Fletch."

He nods. "I know that now, but I was still an immature kid. Did you read my file?"

I still at his words. "File?" I repeat.

"I found it at your place," he admits. "It was my social services records."

I sigh, realising he's caught me out. "I just wanted to know more about you, Fletch. You don't open up."

"Because I don't want you to look at me differently," he explains, sounding frustrated. "There's no big mystery. My mum was shit at being a mum and she gave me up. I bounced from one home to the next because no one could handle me, and then I was put up in that shithole with a man old enough to be Jesus himself. He was a drug dealer on the social services books as a temporary foster carer. Once I went there, they didn't give a shit about me. They knew Terry would be able to keep me in line, and he did. He's the reason I got into drugs and crime, but he's also the reason I ended up meeting The Chaos Demons. And without them, fuck knows where I'd be now."

He takes my hand in his and interlinks our fingers. We both stare at the connection. "We've made such a mess of everything," I say.

"It's not too late to fix it," he says with hope in his voice.

"Isn't it?" I ask, staring down at the water. "We've hurt each other so much."

"I have no secrets, Gem. Yeah, the club does what it needs to, and it's not always the way you'd do things, but you'll never see that side."

"What are you asking me?"

"To give us a chance. We haven't really tried, but when

it's just the two of us, it feels right. Take out all the shit we've done and we're good together."

"What happens when you get arrested and thrown in prison? Because that will happen. You can't try and own these streets and not get caught."

"We're doing alright so far," he says with a smirk.

"I'm serious, Fletch. When you get caught, where will that leave me and Ruby?"

"I won't get caught."

"I can't risk it."

He groans, resting his forehead on the bar and staring out ahead. "Don't you think we've wasted enough time? We could just live day by day, in the moment."

"We have a responsibility now," I argue.

"Fuck's sake, Gemma, stop making excuses. If you don't want to be with me, just tell me straight so I can stop wanting you." He stands. "I can't keep begging you to see what I see. We have a future together, me, you, and Ruby. You just have to say yes."

He walks away, and I stare after him. My heart hurts. Taking a risk on Fletch for a third time is just plain stupid, but everything in me wants to go to him. I love him.

## Fletch

I'M ABOUT to push my helmet on when I hear her call my name. I still and slowly turn, watching as Gemma rushes towards me. "Wait," she calls.

I swore that if she let me leave, that would be it. I'd draw a line under us and move forward. I'd concentrate on being a father to Ruby, and I'd put everything into her.

And now, as Gemma stops in front of me, I'm suddenly lost for words. "I've never been ashamed of you," she says, her breathing rapid from running. "I'm not ashamed to be with you, Fletch, because I do love you. I've always loved you. But being with you scares the shit out of me."

I give a tight nod. "Okay." And I turn away to get on my bike.

"But," she continues, and I pause again, "if I don't at least try, I'll hate myself." I slowly turn back to face her, and she's smiling. "I love you," she adds.

"You're serious?" She nods with a huge grin. "Because I can't take it if you change your mind."

"I won't."

My heart slams hard against my chest, not quite daring to believe what she's telling me. "You know what you're agreeing to?"

"Being your old lady," she whispers with a glint in her eye.

"Being my old lady," I confirm, nodding. I grab her by the waist and pull her into my arms. She laughs, and I swing her around. "For the first time ever, we're doing this out in the open."

"Looks that way."

I kiss her, sliding her down my body. "I think I might just be the happiest man alive right now, Snap."

# CHAPTER 19
### Gemma
*Three months later . . .*

It's the fuss I didn't want, and as Lexi fluffs my hair, I resist the urge to bat her hands away. She's trying to help, and it's nice that we're getting on much better these days, but I told Ruby to make sure they understood I didn't want any fuss.

"Ready?" she asks.

"As I'll ever be," I mutter.

She rolls her eyes and fixes me with a glare. "Try and be a little more enthusiastic."

"She's nervous," Luna cuts in, smiling at me with sympathy.

"I'm not nervous," I hiss, shaking out my shoulders. "You two are making this feel way bigger than it needs to be."

"You're making it official. It's huge." I sigh as Luna opens the bedroom door. "Let's go and claim your man."

Ruby and Fletch are together as usual, and it still brings a smile to my lips whenever I spot them. Being a father seems to have come natural to him, despite his worries, and the pair have a bond that even I struggle to compete with. She announced just last week that she wanted a motorbike, and I know despite my firm reluctance, he's going to get her one. She's already decided she wants to follow his footsteps and work in the garage. I laughed when she told me, knowing how my father would have reacted to the news.

Fletch spots me watching them and holds out his hand, which I take. He tugs me to him and kisses me gently on the lips. "You look amazing."

I glance around the room. "Why are all these people here?"

"I told you, we're celebrating in style. These bikers have come from all our other charters to celebrate with us."

"It's a simple ceremony. We're not even leaving the clubhouse."

He grins. "I know you didn't want anything traditional, but we had to have guests, Snap."

He tugs my dress to expose the tattoo of his name on my collarbone and kisses the spot. He does it often. "You two are gross," Ruby announces, screwing up her nose before heading off to take a seat.

"Are we doing this?" asks Fletch, and I take a deep breath before nodding. He keeps hold of my hand and leads me to the front of the room.

Bikers begin to fill the empty seats that Lexi and Luna carefully set out this afternoon. The vicar rushes over, placing an empty whiskey glass on a nearby table. I smirk, because that could only happen in this club.

"Welcome, everyone," he says jovially. "And thank

you for being here to be a part of this very special union between Cameron and Gemma."

I zone out while he drivels on. I'm so lost in staring at my man, I don't hear his words. Seeing Fletch this happy is worth his weeks of nagging to get me to make us official. Since I agreed to become his old lady, he's done everything possible to ensure I don't back out. He doesn't quite understand that I couldn't leave him now even if I wanted to. He owns me, heart and soul. But even the tattoos weren't enough to settle his worry. So, here we are, tying the knot in a small ceremony.

I realised very quickly that club life isn't so bad. I see why he loves it so much because, even after everything, I've been welcomed by the men here. I sometimes catch Axel and Grizz watching me through suspicious eyes, but Lexi assures me that's how they were with her too, but they soon began to trust her.

And Ruby is so happy here, I could hardly refuse when she begged us to move in. It wasn't a hard decision—being closer to Fletch was what I wanted too.

I shake my head to clear the thoughts and focus back on the vicar, who is now reading off the vows we picked.

The whole thing is over in ten minutes, and as the ring slides onto my finger, I feel a sense of finality. Ruby hands me the flower bouquet I lovingly made from the flowers Luna and I have grown out back. The entire room is filled with the scent of tulips and roses, and when I took photographs to upload to my new website, I was extremely proud to finally be following my dreams.

"Throw my way," Lexi hisses as she passes to stand behind me.

I smirk, closing my eyes and hauling the bouquet over

my shoulder. When I turn, Duchess is holding it with a huge smile on her face. I glance at Fletch, who wiggles his eyebrows in Duke's direction. There must be a story there I don't know about.

"Let's get drunk," Axel shouts, and the room erupts in cheers.

Everyone heads off to the bar, and I go to follow, but Fletch pulls me back, waiting until the room is almost clear before kissing me in a slow, toe-curling kiss. "Thank you," he whispers. "I know this wasn't what you wanted, that you did it for me, and I appreciate it."

"I always wanted to be your wife, Fletch, I just didn't want to do the big white wedding." Apart from a couple close friends, there's no one here for me. I could hardly invite my friends from the police force . . . or my father.

He gently cups my face. "For the first time in my life, I feel complete. I have my own family, and that's something I haven't had in a long time."

I wrap my arms around his neck and kiss him. "Me either."

"I love you, Mrs. Fletcher."

"Forever," I whisper against his lips.

"And ever."

**THE END**

# About the Author

Nicola Jane, a native of Nottinghamshire, England, has always harboured a deep passion for literature. From her formative years, she found solace and excitement within the pages of books, often allowing her imagination to roam freely. As a teenager, she would weave her own narratives through short stories, a practice that ignited her creative spirit.

After a hiatus, Nicola returned to writing as a means to liberate the stories swirling within her mind. It wasn't until approximately five years ago that she summoned the courage to share her work with the world. Since then, Nicola has dedicated herself tirelessly to crafting poignant, drama-infused romance tales. Her stories are imbued with a sense of realism, tackling challenging themes with a deft touch.

Outside of her literary pursuits, Nicola finds joy in the company of her husband and two teenage children. They share moments of laughter and bonding that enrich her life beyond the realm of words.

Nicola Jane has many books from motorcycle romance to mafia romance, all can be found on Amazon and in Kindle Unlimited.

# Follow Nicola Here...

I love to hear from my readers and if you'd like to get in touch, you can find me here . . .

My Facebook Page
My Facebook Readers Group
Bookbub
Instagram
Goodreads
Amazon
I'm also on Tiktok